A PALETTE FULL OF LOVERS

A REVERSE HAREM ROMANCE

THE ART OF HAVING IT ALL
BOOK TWO

SADIE WATERS

For Ms Divine

CONTENTS

GOODBYE IS THE LONELIEST WORD

Harper

Three months. That's how long it's been since my life became a balancing act between love, ambition, and enough sexual pleasure to power a reality show. I'm basically the poster child for chaos, except now it comes with a wardrobe upgrade and a much better skincare routine. Unfortunately, it hasn't come with a bigger closet.

These days, I basically have to shove myself into my closet head on just to squeeze through the tight space between the rows. With all the designer dresses Damien's sent me, I'm having a hard time finding space. McKenzy says I should just get rid of all my old clothes, but it's not like I'm going to lounge around in our apartment in Dolce and Gabbana.

"Rich people problems," she always says with a sigh whenever I complain about the closet space.

Of course, I'm still far from rich. But I'm definitely in a better place than I was when this all began. My paintings have sold so well, I've been able to put aside rent money for the rest of the year. It's such a relief knowing that I can just focus on my painting without stressing about when or how the money will come. For that, I'm also very grateful to Damien.

Rafe has also introduced me to some very influential people who've asked for commissions. I'm regularly struggling to keep up with the demand, which is not a problem I ever thought I'd have so early in my career. Take that, Mom and Dad!

Tonight, McKenzy's sprawled across our couch, wearing yesterday's leggings, eating peanut butter out of the jar with a serving spoon. She's my rock, though more accurately, I'd have to say she's my chaos twin. The yin to my yang. After all, none of this would have even happened without her; I definitely wouldn't have started dating for money without her intervention. She watches me pace in front of my stuffed closet while I wait for divine wardrobe intervention.

After hearing me groan for the umpteenth time, she pokes her head into my room.

"You've been standing there for twenty minutes," she says. "Are you thinking about outfits or having an existential crisis?"

"Both," I admit, because lying to McKenzy is pointless.

"Rafe leaves tomorrow, doesn't he?" she asks, licking peanut butter off the spoon.

"Yup." My voice goes higher than usual, which is a dead giveaway of how I feel about that.

"And you still don't know if you're going with him."

"Nope."

She sets down the peanut butter, all serious now. "Do you wanna go?"

2

SELFISH SOLUTION

I wake up to the sound of Rafe singing very off-key to some '90s alt-rock song in the kitchen. It takes me a second to remember where I am, why my legs are tangled in a sheet that smells like him, and why my heart already aches before my feet even hit the floor.

Today's the day.

I sit up, blinking at the sunlight pouring in through the half-open blinds. Rafe's room is packed up, a cardboard box labeled *TROPHIES + RANDOM SHIT* sits by the door, and his dresser drawers hang open, mostly empty. It feels wrong, like the room itself is bracing for the goodbye we're both pretending isn't coming.

I pull on one of his T-shirts, feeling vulnerable and pathetic, and follow the smell of coffee into the kitchen. Rafe is standing at the stove, shirtless, flipping pancakes like a domestic god who doesn't know his own biceps should be illegal.

"Morning, sleepyhead." He grins, flashing me that too-charming smile that got me into this mess in the first place.

"You're making pancakes?" I ask, leaning against the counter.

He shrugs. "Seemed appropriate for a last breakfast."

"Don't say *last breakfast* like we're on death row."

He flips a pancake dramatically. "Fine. Our *temporary farewell feast*. Better?"

"Marginally." I steal a piece of bacon from the plate beside him. "But you still owe me emotional compensation for making me cry in my sleep last night."

His smile fades for half a second. "You cried?"

"Only a little." I try to lighten the mood. "Probably just allergic to you leaving."

He turns down the stove and pulls me into his arms, flour-dusted fingers tracing patterns down my spine. "You could still change your mind," he whispers.

"I can't." My voice cracks just enough for him to hear. "My life is here. My job. My friends."

"Your other boyfriends," he teases with no real malice, though the ache of separation still hangs heavy between us.

I cup his face, forcing him to look at me. "I love you. That doesn't change just because we live in different states."

"I know," he says, but his voice breaks with emotion.

Breakfast is quieter than usual. We sit cross-legged on the floor because the table's already loaded into the moving truck. The pancakes are slightly burned, but the bacon is perfect, and the silence is way too loud.

"So," Rafe says after a few bites. "You'll visit?"

"Of course," I answer quickly.

"And you'll call?"

"Constantly."

"And you'll send nudes?"

"I'll consider it."

He grins, but it doesn't quite reach his eyes.

The drive back to my apartment is full of 'remember when' stories —the time we got caught making out under the bleachers, the time we nearly broke up over a miscommunication about

prom, the time I painted a portrait of him and made his nose too big. Every story feels like we're folding memories into tiny paper cranes to tuck in our pockets.

Outside my building, he kisses me like he's memorizing the shape of my mouth. "This isn't goodbye," I say.

"Just see you later," he finishes.

I stand on the sidewalk watching him drive away, and when his car turns the corner, I finally let myself cry for real.

Inside, McKenzy is sprawled on the couch, scrolling TikTok. "Welcome home, heartbreak queen," she says without looking up.

"Thanks." I flop onto the armrest. "It's been a morning."

"You want distraction or commiseration?"

"Distraction, please."

McKenzy grins like the devil herself. "Perfect. Because you left your phone here last night and the Whitney Gallery called."

My heart skips a beat as I reach for my forgotten cell phone, wondering how I managed to do that and didn't even miss it. Guess I was distracted. "The one in Chicago?"

"The very same." She tosses her phone at me. "They want one of your paintings for their next show."

I scream. McKenzy screams. The neighbor upstairs bangs on the floor to tell us to shut up.

"You're kidding!" I clutch her shoulders. "Which painting?"

"They said they'll leave it up to you. They want something bold, something that shows who you are."

"Holy shit." I drop onto the couch. "I have no idea what to send."

"Don't worry. I've already narrowed it down to the top three options." McKenzy pulls up a folder on her phone. "Option one, your abstract of the night sky. Option two, the messy self-portrait you made after that wine binge. Option three, the half-naked one of Rafe."

"Absolutely not the Rafe one," I say immediately. "He doesn't need to be immortalized that way."

"You're no fun."

Before I can fully process the gallery news, my phone buzzes again.

Damien: Dinner tonight?

"This is your life," she says dramatically. "Hot men summoning you to expensive dinners like you're a duchess."

"It's exhausting. And yes, I love it."

"What's he sending this time?" she asks.

"Probably something ridiculous."

Five minutes later, the doorbell rings. The delivery guy hands over a box so sleek it belongs in a Bond movie. Inside is a dress made entirely of sinful intentions, a pair of heels so high I'll need a spotter, and a bracelet that's probably worth more than my entire art collection.

McKenzy whistles. "You really do live in a romance novel."

"Tell me about it." I giggle, holding the dress against my body.

I check the time and realize I have a couple of hours to paint before I need to start getting ready for whatever ridiculously grand adventure Damien has planned for me tonight.

I've sent Harper dozens of dresses since we started our romance. Half of them were chosen to make her feel like a goddess. The other half were designed specifically to make me want to bend her over the nearest surface the second I saw her. Though, truthfully, every dress has had that effect so far.

Tonight's dress is absolutely no exception.

When she steps outside, my cock twitches in my slacks like I'm a fucking teenager. The slit runs so high I can see the lace band at the top of her thigh, and the neckline is one deep breath away from showing me exactly how excited she is for tonight.

"Holy shit, little red bird," I say, opening the car door for her. "Are you trying to kill me before we even make it to dinner?"

Her lips curve in that wicked smile that always makes my pulse spike. "You picked it, baby. Don't blame me if you can't handle it."

I guide her into the car, my hand staying on her thigh a little longer than necessary, fingers brushing bare skin. She shivers under my touch, and I know the game's already started.

The restaurant is all understated luxury with soft music, low lighting, and wait staff that knows my drink order before I sit down. I own half the room, or at least, I've bought drinks for everyone important in it. But the only person worth paying attention to tonight is Harper.

She knows it, too.

Her foot slides up my calf before we even order drinks, and her smile turns sweet when the waiter asks if we'd like champagne.

"Champagne sounds perfect," she says, eyes locked on mine.

Tease.

"You're staring," she points out when the waiter steps away.

"Can you blame me?" My gaze drops to the neckline of her dress then back up to the smirk playing on her lips. "The most beautiful woman in the room is sitting across from me, wearing a dress I'm about five seconds away from ripping off."

She bites her lip, shifting slightly in her chair, and I swear I can hear the soft brush of her thighs rubbing together.

"Bold move," she teases.

"Only if it's not true."

She tries to play it cool, but there's a flush rising in her cheeks. I know that look. She's already getting wet, and we haven't even ordered appetizers.

Dinner is a blur of seafood, flirting, and the kind of dirty whispers that would make the surrounding tables blush if they could hear us. I keep my hand on her thigh under the table the entire meal, tracing patterns on her skin, slipping higher every time she tries to talk about something serious.

She's trying to tell me something about Rafe, about how worried she is about the distance, but I can't focus with her legs spread just enough to let my fingers ghost along the edge of her panties.

"Baby," she hisses, swatting my hand away with zero conviction.

"Hmm?" I smile innocently.

"I'm trying to talk to you."

"And I'm trying to figure out if you wore these panties for me, or if you're hoping Rafe gets a peek later."

She rolls her eyes, but her breath catches when I press my fingers a little harder.

"You're impossible."

"And you love it."

I solve her problem the same way I solve all of life's problems. With money and charm.

"Why don't I just buy you your own apartment in San Francisco?" I suggest, sipping my whiskey. "That way you're not living in Rafe's space, and I can come visit whenever I feel like it."

She blinks at me like I just offered to buy her the moon. "You'd really do that?"

"Little red bird, I'd buy you the whole damn city if it meant you'd stop worrying," I tell her honestly, though the apartment really is selfishly for me.

Her foot slides higher up my calf, her fingers tracing the stem of her glass.

"I don't deserve you."

"Trust me, darling, it's the other way around," I argue, my voice low and hot.

We barely make it to the car before my hand is under her dress again, sliding up her thigh, fingers slipping beneath lace.

"Damien," she whispers, glancing at the driver.

"He's seen plenty before." I kiss her neck, fingers pressing just enough to feel the heat between her legs. "Besides, you like the idea of getting caught."

She shudders, biting back a moan as I stroke her through her panties.

"Be good," I murmur, "or I'll make you come in this car before we even get home."

She spreads her legs wider in answer. I put up the divider between us and the driver and press her as far as I can before she breaks.

The penthouse is dark and quiet when we step inside, but we don't need lights. I know every inch of this place, and more importantly, I know every inch of her.

Harper walks straight to the window, looking out at the skyline like she's already picturing her new life in San Francisco.

"What do you think your apartment should have?" I ask, stepping behind her, hands sliding around her waist. "Big windows? A balcony?"

She leans back into me, her ass pressing against my growing erection.

"A big kitchen," she says, her voice all sweet innocence.

"Why?"

"So I can bend over the counter and let you fuck me while the sun comes up."

I groan, biting her shoulder gently. "You're killing me, little red bird."

She turns in my arms, fingers already working my shirt buttons. "Then stop talking and show me what I'm worth."

I pin her to the window, the city lights painting her skin in gold and silver, and slide my hand between her thighs. Her panties are already soaked. My good girl, always so ready for me.

"Look at you," I whisper. "All this for me?"

"All for you."

I sink to my knees, kissing up the inside of her thigh, pushing her dress higher with each kiss. When I reach her panties, I tug them down with my teeth, savoring the shiver that runs through her.

"Hold on to the glass," I order. "Don't move."

She does as she's told, hands flat against the window, her breath fogging the glass as I press my tongue to her clit. This is the position she was in the first time I took her.

"God," she whimpers, thighs trembling.

I pin her hips, taking my time, teasing her until she's begging, until her knees are about to give out.

"Please," she whispers. "Please, Damien."

I slide two fingers inside her, curling them just right, my mouth never leaving her clit. She comes hard, crying out against the glass, her body shuddering as I hold her up.

I stand, licking my fingers clean, and press my body against hers.

"That's one," I murmur in her ear. "Think you can handle another before bed?"

She nods, still breathless. "Yes…"

I walk her backward to the bedroom, letting her dress fall to the floor on the way, already planning exactly how I'm going to make her beg next.

Because my little red bird deserves nothing less.

3

———————

DANCE WITH ME

The afternoon sun pours through the studio windows, spilling delicate golden light across the floor. My latest painting is sitting on the easel, half-finished, all the colors still swirling together, but I'm not satisfied with the result. I dip my brush into my favorite cobalt blue, dragging it over the canvas, blending it into the burnt orange sunset I'm trying to capture.

It's *almost* there. Almost perfect.

I've been at this for hours. My back aches, my fingers are speckled with dried paint, and I've barely moved since lunchtime. I'm so focused until McKenzy texts me a meme about a disastrous DIY project. At that I laugh, stretching out my stiff shoulders before turning back to the painting.

That's when my phone rings.

I consider ignoring it, until I see Tomas's name flashing across the screen.

I bite my lip, warmth spreading through my chest as I answer. "Hola, Profe."

"Hola, preciosa," Tomas's smooth, accented voice flows through the line like a slow dance, making my pulse skip. "Are you terribly busy tonight?"

I glance at my painting, the light shifting as the sun lowers in the sky. "Define *terribly busy*."

Tomas chuckles, and the sound sends a shiver down my spine. "I thought you might like a break. Would you care to go dancing with me tonight?"

My stomach does that ridiculous flip it always makes when one of my men calls, and my hips already want to sway at the thought of moving with him. Most importantly, I imagine his hands on my hips, sliding just a little too low to be appropriate.

"You know I never say no to salsa," I tease, setting my brush down and stretching my free arm over my head.

"I was hoping you'd say that," he murmurs. "I'll pick you up at eight. Wear something that makes you feel irresistible."

"I always feel irresistible."

Tomas chuckles. "I won't argue with that, *mi preciosa*."

We hang up, and I stand there for a moment, phone clutched to my chest, grinning like an idiot.

A night of salsa dancing with Tomas is exactly what I need. Hopefully it will help me get out of my head enough to come back to this piece with fresh eyes.

I abandon my painting for the evening, heading straight for the bathroom. The hot water cascades over me, washing away the remnants of paint and exhaustion. My thoughts drift as I shampoo my hair, imagining the way Tomas will look at me tonight... the way he always looks at me, like he's waiting for the perfect moment to devour me.

After my shower, I wrap myself in a fluffy towel and rifle through my closet. For once, I know exactly what I want to wear. I grab the red salsa dress I bought specifically for a dancing date Tomas and I had a few weeks ago. It has become my secret weapon. The fabric clings like a second skin, the neckline daring but elegant, the slit running so high up my thigh it could be considered scandalous.

Tomas loves me in this dress. I smirk to myself, slipping it on, the silky fabric hugging my curves.

Right on cue, McKenzy waltzes into my room, flopping onto my bed like she owns the place. "That's a sexy dress," she says salaciously. "Are you planning to set some poor man's heart on fire tonight?"

"Maybe not fire." I laugh, adjusting the straps. "Tomas and I are just going dancing at a salsa club."

McKenzy lets out a low whistle. "And you're wearing *that*? Girl, he doesn't stand a *chance*."

"That's the plan." I wink at her in the mirror.

She props herself up on her elbows, watching as I pick out my jewelry.

"You know, I probably should be jealous of your ridiculous love life, but honestly, I'm just impressed."

I grin at her in the mirror. "You and me both."

McKenzy sits up, grabbing my setting spray and spritzing my face like a professional makeup artist. "Seriously, though. You have four ridiculously hot men wrapped around your finger. How are they not clawing each other's eyes out?"

"They're too busy competing for my attention," I say smugly.

"That's… queen shit." She nods approvingly.

I laugh, shaking my head. "You know what? I'll put in a good word for you with the next sexy billionaire I meet."

McKenzy sighs dramatically. "That's all I ask."

Just as I finish my lipstick, a bold red to match the dress, my phone buzzes again.

Tomas: I'm outside, preciosa.

My stomach flips again.

McKenzy peeks over my shoulder. "He didn't even text 'here' like a normal person. He's so suave, it's disgusting."

"It really is," I agree, grabbing my clutch.

She follows me to the kitchen, pouring two quick shots of tequila. "A new pre-dance tradition," she declares, handing me one.

I smirk, clinking my glass against hers. "To making Tomas sweat."

"To making Tomas *suffer*."

We down the shots, and warmth spreads through me instantly.

I barely have time to grab my heels before the buzzer sounds. I step into them, smooth down my dress, and open the door.

And there he is, standing in the hallway, leaning casually against the doorframe, looking like the manifestation of every sinful thought I've ever had. He's wearing a crisp black button-down shirt, with the sleeves rolled up a bit, to tease at his forearms, the top buttons undone just enough to show the top of his chest. His dark hair is perfectly styled, his warm brown eyes drinking me in from head to toe.

And that *smirk*.

Dios mío.

Tomas's gaze sweeps over me slowly, like he's savoring every inch. "Preciosa," he sighs out in amazement.

I tilt my head playfully. "Something wrong?"

He exhales sharply, shaking his head. "You are going to be the death of me."

I lean against the doorframe, mirroring his stance. "Well, at least you'll die happy."

Tomas chuckles, stepping closer, his fingers grazing my waist as he pulls me in. "Very happy." His lips brush my cheek, then hover near my ear. "Are you ready?"

"For you? Always."

He finds my hand, his grip firm, warm, familiar.

As we step into the night, I can already feel the electricity sparking between us. Dancing with Tomas is never *just* dancing. And tonight I intend to drive him absolutely wild.

Tomas

I'M STILL NOT USED TO THE FEELING OF ANTICIPATION CURLING IN MY stomach when I knock on Harper's door, knowing she's behind it. It's been months now, but my pulse always kicks up the second I know I'm about to see her.

She opened the door and just like that, every rational thought evaporated. Dios mío.

She's wearing *the dress*, the red one that clings like it was painted on, the one that makes every man in the club lose focus the second she walks by. But right now, there's no one to see her but me, and it feels like a private blessing.

"Stop staring," Harper teases once we're out on the sidewalk, spinning just enough to make the hem flirt with her thighs. "Unless you want to skip dancing entirely."

"Tempting," I admit, stepping closer. "But you promised me a dance."

She grins, sliding her arms around my neck. "Then you better dance me right out of this dress."

The drive to the club is mundane, familiar. We've made this trip so many times now, I know every curve in the road, every street lamp that flickers just before we pass. What's new is the weight in my chest, the thing I've been meaning to tell her.

I wait until we're at a red light. "Carmen's been texting me."

Harper glances over, her brow lifting. "Seriously?"

"She's feeling… what's the word in English?" I stop to think as I try to quickly translate in my head. "Nostalgic, I think."

"For what? Making your life miserable?"

I can't help but laugh at the heat in her voice. "Maybe," I say with a shrug

Harper leans back in her seat, her hand running up my thigh dangerously. "What does she want?"

"No sé. I think she saw one of those pictures you posted from the gallery event, the one where you're in that gold dress."

"Oh." Harper smiles. "So, she's jealous."

"Extremely."

"Can't blame her." She bats her lashes dramatically. "I am pretty irresistible."

"You are," I say softly. "But it's not just that."

Her smile falters. "What do you mean?"

I exhale slowly, turning onto the street where the club awaits, neon lights spilling onto the sidewalk. "Carmen has this bad habit of wanting things she can't have."

"And you think she wants you back now?" Harper's voice is playful, but I can hear the edge.

"No," I say immediately. "I think she wants to ruin this, to ruin you, before we have a chance to become something real."

Harper shrugs one bare shoulder. "Let her try."

Inside the club, the music wraps around us instantly, with its fast, pulsing, irresistible rhythm. This place is ours, the one spot where I can lose myself completely in her.

I take her hand and pull her onto the floor before she has time to think. The beat finds us first, my palm at her back, her body fitting against mine, my knee sliding between her thighs as we move.

Harper is a natural dancer now, but she wasn't always. I remember the first time I brought her here, the way she tripped over her own feet, the way she laughed instead of blushing, the way she held onto me like I was her lifeline.

Now, she doesn't need saving. She moves with me like we've been doing this for years, our bodies speaking their own language. Every touch is a tease, every step a promise.

"You're showing off tonight," I murmur, spinning her out and back again.

"Maybe." She smiles up at me. "I've got a lot to show."

I slide my hand lower, my fingers grazing the edge of her dress, ready to take it off.

We dance for hours, stopping only for drink breaks where we lean against the bar, breathing hard and grinning like teenagers sneaking out past curfew. Harper's hair sticks to her neck, her skin flushed, and all I can think about is getting her alone.

By the time the music slows, I can barely think straight. My hands stay on her waist longer than they should, my fingers digging into the soft fabric of her dress.

"Helena," I murmur, using her name from my Spanish class, my lips brushing the shell of her ear. "Let's get out of here."

She nods, breathless, her hands sliding down my chest. "Take me home, Profe."

Back at my apartment, I'm barely able to get the door open before I'm on her. Her back hits the wall, her leg hooked over my hip, my hands full of her curves. She tastes like rum and lime and desire, and I'm drunk on all of it.

"Every time we dance," I murmur against her lips, "it makes me want to take you right there on the floor."

"Why didn't you?" she teases, her fingers already tugging my shirt from my waistband.

"Because you deserve better than a sticky floor and an audience." I kiss my way down her neck, nipping at her pulse. "But here? In my home? You're all mine, Helena."

She sighs into my mouth, and I scoop her up, her legs wrapping around my waist as I carry her to my bedroom. She's light in my arms, but the weight of her means everything.

In my room, the moonlight catches her skin, making her glow as I set her on the edge of the bed. I step back, letting my eyes roam, taking my time to drink her in.

"Take off your dress," I say softly.

She stands slowly, holding my gaze as she reaches for the zipper. The red fabric slips down her body like water, pooling at her feet. Underneath, she wears only a tiny scrap of black lace, and my self-control officially ceases to exist.

"*Eres una obra de arte,*" I whisper. A work of art.

"You're wearing too much," she replies, stepping closer, her fingers working the buttons of my shirt.

Her hands are warm, familiar, and when her fingertips brush my skin, my breath stutters.

She undresses me like she's unwrapping a present, and when my pants hit the floor, she drops to her knees.

"Helena," I moan, already anticipating the feel of her soft lips around me.

"Shh," she murmurs, her hand wrapping around my cock. "I want to taste you, Profe."

I lean back against the wall, fingers tangling in her hair as she takes me into her mouth. Her tongue is sin and salvation, her lips soft and wicked, and I swear I see stars.

"Dios," I groan, my head falling back. "You are too good at that."

She hums around me, her free hand stroking what she can't fit in her mouth, and I know I won't last if she keeps this up.

"Helena, stop." I gently tug her hair. "I want to be inside you."

She stands, her body flushed, her lips swollen. "Then take me, Profe."

I lay her back on the bed, sliding her panties down her legs. She's already glistening, her thighs parting to welcome me.

I sink into her slowly, watching her face, the way her lips part, the way her nails dig into my arms.

"*Tan perfecta*," I murmur, thrusting deeper.

"Mas, Profe," she begs, her heels digging into my back. " More. Please."

I give her more. Harder. Faster. I lose myself in her, in the way she moans my name, in the heat of her body wrapped around me.

Her climax hits first, her body clenching tight, pulling me over the edge with her. I spill into her with a groan, my forehead pressed to hers, our breaths mingling.

We lay there tangled together, her fingers tracing lazy patterns on my back.

"Dancing always ends this way for us," I murmur.

She grins, her smile soft and sated. "It's the reason I keep showing up."

And just like that, I'm ready to dance with her all over again.

4

CARNIVALS AND OTHER RIDES

THE PAINTING IS MASSIVE, MUCH BIGGER THAN ANYTHING I'VE EVER sent to a gallery before. It's propped against the wall, and every time I glance at it, my heart does a weird little flutter. This is the piece I'm sending to The Whitney Gallery. If I overthink it, I'll keep making changes, trying to make it perfect. But art isn't about perfection, right?

I don't know if it's good enough. I don't know if I'm good enough. But I know I've poured every piece of me into it… my chaos, my love, my fear, my hope. It's all there, dripping down the canvas in colors that feel like my soul spread wide open.

What I do know for sure is that I can't shove something this big into the back of an Uber. And the car McKenzy and I share is barely bigger than a shoe. So, naturally, I call Scott, the only person I know with a pickup truck.

"Hey, babe." He answers on the second ring, his voice warm and relaxed. "What's up?"

"I need a favor."

"Name it."

"Can you bring your truck over and help me take my painting to have it shipped? It's kind of huge."

Scott laughs, that low, easy sound that always makes me smile. "What'd I tell you about going big?"

"That size matters?"

"Damn right." I can practically hear his grin through the phone. "I'll be there in twenty."

Scott shows up wearing faded jeans, work boots, and a flannel that fits entirely too well for my peace of mind. His hair is a little messy, like he's just come in from the field, and it takes all my self-restraint not to say "screw the painting" and fuck him right now.

Scott whistles low, pulling me out of my illicit train of thought. "Damn, Harper. This is gorgeous."

"Thanks," I mumble, feeling both a little vulnerable and a lot turned on.

He lifts the painting like it weighs nothing, which is both impressive and slightly infuriating considering it took both me and McKenzy to prop it against the wall earlier. We wrap it up so it won't get ruined on the trip.

"Truck's out front," Scott says. "Let's get this masterpiece on the road."

The drive to the shipping center is easy, even with the painting taking up most of the truck bed. I sit sideways in the passenger seat, my feet tucked under me, watching Scott drive. His hands are steady on the wheel, calloused and strong, and I can't help but think about all the magical things those hands can do.

"So, you busy tomorrow night?" Scott asks casually.

I tilt my head. "Why? Got a hot date?"

"Thinking about it." He glances at me with a grin. "There's a carnival in town. Thought maybe you'd wanna go."

I gasp dramatically. "Scott Bauer, are you asking me on a date?"

He chuckles. "Yeah, I'm asking," he answers with the confidence of a man who knows he won't be rejected.

"You know I can't say no to a carnival."

"That's what I was counting on."

After we drop the painting off, we grab milkshakes at the diner down the street, strawberry for me, chocolate for him, and sit in the bed of his truck watching the sunset like a scene straight out of a country music video.

"You're really excited about this gallery, aren't you?" Scott asks.

"I'm terrified," I admit. "But yeah. It feels big, like maybe the most important thing I'll ever do in my life."

"It *is* big." He nudges me with his shoulder. "You're gonna kill it. But there are definitely bigger things on the horizon."

"I hope so," I say self-consciously, feeling like I've already gotten more out of life than I ever thought possible. Sometimes it feels selfish to wish for more.

"There are." There's no doubt in his voice, just solid, unshakable belief.

Scott

It doesn't matter how many times I've seen her, how many times I've held her, how many times I've buried myself so deep inside her I swear I could see heaven. Every time Harper opens the door, it hits me like a gut punch.

Even in just jeans and a T-shirt, she's the most beautiful thing I've ever seen. Her hair's pulled back into a messy ponytail, little strands curling around her face, and her smile… God, that smile could knock me flat if I wasn't already leaning against my truck to keep my balance.

"Hey, sugar," I say, drinking her in.

"Hey, yourself," she teases, sliding into the passenger seat.

The scent of her, lavender and something soft and warm, fills the cab instantly. I want to lean over, pull her into my lap, and forget the carnival entirely, but I'm trying to be a gentleman tonight. "Trying" being the operative word.

"Ready for some funnel cake and rigged games?" I ask, putting the truck in gear.

She grins. "You know it."

I reach across the console, my hand resting on her thigh as I drive. Every time I have my hands on her, it's like reminding myself she's real. She's here. She's mine–and I don't mind sharing her one bit as long as I get to have her in my life.

The carnival's all bright lights and laughter, smells like sugar and frying oil, and Harper fits in perfectly, bright, sweet, and irresistible. I feed her bites of my fried pickle, and she feeds me bites of her funnel cake until her fingers are dusted with powdered sugar, and I can't help myself. I take her hand and suck each fingertip into my mouth.

"Scott," she laughs, a flush rising in her cheeks.

"What? You taste better than the food."

I win her a stuffed llama at the ring toss, impressing her with my perfect aim. When we ride the Ferris wheel, her head on my shoulder, and her hand tangled in mine, I realize I'd do just about anything to keep her looking this happy.

"Hey," I say softly as we climb down from the ride and head to the cotton candy stand. "I wanted to ask you something."

She tilts her head, curious.

"My great-grandma's turning a hundred in a couple weeks. Big family party, all the cousins and uncles, the works. I'd love to have you there."

Her whole face lights up, and I swear I fall a little harder. "Of course I'll come. Your family's awesome."

"They love you, sugar. Hell, I think they'd adopt you if I let 'em."

After she finishes her cotton candy, we head back to my truck, her hand still in mine, the llama tucked under her other arm, and it's the easiest, happiest night I've had in longer than I can remember.

Back at my place, Harper kicks off her shoes the second we walk inside, already looking at home.

"Whiskey?" I ask, heading for the kitchen.

She nods, following me. "You always know how to end a perfect night."

I pour us each a glass of the good stuff because Harper deserves the best, and we settle onto the couch. But with her next to me, her knee brushing mine, her lips still pink and sticky from the cotton candy, I can't sit still. My fingers find their way to her thigh, tracing little circles just under the hem of her jeans.

"You've got powdered sugar in your hair," I murmur, brushing a strand behind her ear.

"Carnival casualty," she says, smiling up at me.

I lean in, close enough that her breath catches. "You look sweet enough to eat."

She licks her bottom lip, and I'm done for.

We're kissing before either of us even sets our glasses down, her hand in my hair, my hand on her hips, tugging her into my lap. The soft little noises she makes, those breathy gasps and low moans, drive me wild. I want to slow this down, savor her, show her how much I've missed her.

"Shower?" I suggest, my lips brushing her ear.

Her whole body shivers. "Together?"

"Of course."

I lead her to the bathroom, flipping the water on hot until steam curls around us. I strip her slowly, peeling off her T-shirt and jeans like I'm unwrapping a gift I plan to take my sweet time enjoying. Her body's already flushed from the heat, her skin dewy and soft, and I swear I could get off just looking at her.

"Get in," I say, tugging my own shirt off.

By the time I step in behind her, she's already slick and wet. I press myself against her back, my hands curving around her waist, and let my mouth wander down her neck, her shoulder, that soft spot just below her ear.

"Scott…." She gasps as her head falls back against my chest.

"What, sugar?"

"Touch me."

I slide my hand between her legs, fingers parting her folds, and she's already so wet I groan into her ear. "You're perfect."

I tease her, circling her clit, dipping two fingers inside her, then back to her clit until she's trembling against me.

"Come for me, baby," I whisper, my other hand cupping her breast, thumb stroking her nipple.

She cries out, her back arching, and I catch her, holding her steady as an orgasm ripples through her. God, she's beautiful like this. But I need more. I need her.

I lift her into my arms, her legs wrapping around my waist, and hastily dry us both off before I carry her, still flushed, to my bed.

I settle her onto the mattress, her skin still damp and glistening from the shower, her hair curling at the ends. She looks up at me, her aquamarine eyes sparkling with mischief and something softer, something she doesn't always let me see. Vulnerability. Trust.

"Come here," she whispers, reaching for me.

I lower myself over her, bracing my weight on my forearms so I don't crush her, and the second our bodies align, her curves molding perfectly to my muscles, I know I'm a goner. I kiss her softly at first, tasting the sweetness of her lips, the lingering hint of cotton candy still clinging to her tongue. Her fingers tangle in my damp hair, tugging me closer, deeper, until the kiss turns hungry and desperate.

I slide my hand down her side, over the curve of her waist, pausing to cup her hip. My thumb strokes lazy circles into her skin, just to feel her shiver beneath me. God, I love the way she reacts, her breath hitching, her legs parting just enough to invite me between them.

"You're so damn beautiful, Harper," I murmur against her lips. "You know that?"

She smiles up at me, her cheeks flushed, her lips already kiss-swollen. "You're not so bad yourself, farmer boy."

I chuckle, but the sound fades as my fingers slip between her thighs. She's so wet already, still soft and swollen from the pleasure I gave her in the shower. My cock twitches in response, desperate to sink into all that slick heat, but I want to take my time with her first. I want to memorize every sigh, every shiver, every whispered plea.

"Scott," she breathes, her hips arching into my hand. "Please."

I stroke her, parting her folds, my fingers sliding through the evidence of just how badly she wants this… wants me. That does something primal to me, knowing this beautiful, incredible woman wants me as much as I want her.

"Always so ready for me," I whisper, slipping two fingers inside her.

She gasps, her nails biting into my shoulders, her back arching off the bed. I curl my fingers, searching for that perfect spot, and then I find the place that makes her cry out my name.

"Right there?" I murmur, pressing a kiss to her throat.

"Yes," she stammers, her legs trembling.

I keep my fingers moving, slow and deep, my thumb circling her clit, and it's not long before she's falling apart for me all over again. Her breathless cries fill the room. I love watching her come, the way her body goes tight, her face flushes, her mouth falling open in a silent scream. She's so damn beautiful, it almost hurts.

"Scott," she pants when she finally comes down, her eyes glassy and soft. "I need you."

I line myself up, the thick head of my cock brushing against her entrance, and even after all the times we've done this before, she's still so damn tight I have to grit my teeth to keep from losing it right then and there.

"You okay, sugar?" I ask, sliding in just an inch.

She nods, her hands running up my back. "Please."

That's all the invitation I need.

I push into her slowly, inch by inch, letting her feel every bit of me stretching her open. I've always been careful with Harper, knowing I'm bigger than she's used to, but tonight, she seems to crave every inch of me, her hips rising to meet mine, her nails scratching down my back, urging me deeper.

"God, sugar," I groan, fully inside her. "You feel so damn good."

She whimpers, wrapping her legs around my waist, her ankles locking at the small of my back. "Move," she begs.

I do. Slowly at first, then faster, deeper, until we're both panting, skin slick with sweat, bodies moving together like we were made for each other. Her hands grip my ass, pulling me harder against her, and I swear I see stars.

"Touch yourself," I whisper, needing to watch her unravel while I'm inside her.

She does, her fingers finding her clit, and the sight alone almost undoes me. But I hold on, thrusting deep and steady, whispering filthy praise in her ear. I tell how good she feels, how beautiful she looks, how I'll never get enough of her.

"Come for me, Harper," I urge, my thumb brushing over her nipple. "Let me feel you."

She cries out my name, her inner muscles clenching tight around me, and that's all it takes to send me over the edge right behind her. I empty inside her with a groan, my body shuddering from the force of it.

We collapse together, tangled and breathless, my heart pounding so hard I'm sure she can feel it against her chest.

For a long moment, neither of us speaks. We just lie there, limbs tangled, breath mingling, until finally, she breaks the silence with a soft laugh.

"What's so funny?" I ask, brushing her hair off her damp forehead.

"I just…." She breathes, smiling up at me. "I really love carnivals."

5

GO TEAM!

HARPER

MY PHONE BUZZES ON THE NIGHTSTAND, AND I NEARLY KNOCK OVER A half-empty mug of coffee trying to grab it.

Damien: *Pack your bags, little red bird. My jet leaves at 10:00 A.M. on Friday.*

I grin, biting my lip, and another message pops in before I can reply.

Damien: *And bring the other two along. I suppose they can sit with the peasants in the back.*

Scott: *I'm taller than you.*

Tomas: *And I'm more charming.*

Damien: *But I'm richer.*

I can't stop laughing as the group chat explodes with the kind of snarky chaos that has somehow become my new normal.

Scott: *Don't care. I'm bringing snacks.*

Tomas: *Do not let Scott choose the snacks. I beg you.*

Damien: *Fine. I'll stock the jet myself. Only the finest artisanal chips and caviar-flavored popcorn.*

Rafe: *Wait. What's happening?*

I snort. Rafe's been so laser-focused on training camp he's missed half the group texts lately.

Me: *We're all coming to your first home game, baby.*

Rafe: *What? How? Who's "we all"?*

Damien: *Me, little red bird, her farmer boy, and her academic boyfriend.*

Scott: *We have names, you know?*

Damien: *Not on my jet you don't.*

Rafe: *This is insane.*

Me: *I know! I can't wait.*

I set the phone down, my heart thudding with excitement. This is really happening–all four of my guys in one city, for a whole weekend. My life is a circus, and I wouldn't have it any other way.

The next day, McKenzy appears in my doorway, holding a Diet Coke in one hand and her phone in the other, watching me as I pack.

"So," she says with a grin, "how does it feel to be the luckiest bitch alive?"

"Ridiculous," I say, tossing a dress into my suitcase without even looking at it. "Completely, outrageously ridiculous."

She plops down on my bed, her legs crossed under her like a kid at a sleepover. "Walk me through this again because the logistics alone are giving me stress hives."

I flop down beside her. "Okay, so Damien's flying us all out on his jet because apparently that's just a thing people do when they have a fuck-ton of money."

"Obviously."

"But he has to leave early for some fancy art thing in London. So Scott and Tomas are staying at a hotel."

"The hotel Damien owns?" McKenzy asks, her eyebrows arched so high they practically touch her hairline.

"Of course."

"And you–" She points a finger at me like a detective solving a case. "You get to stay in the fancy-ass apartment Damien bought you, the one walking distance from Rafe's place."

"Bingo."

She sighs dramatically. "God, I hope I come back as you in my next life."

"Careful what you wish for," I warn, tossing a pair of heels toward the suitcase. I miss. "My life is held together with duct tape and orgasms."

McKenzy cackles so hard she nearly chokes on her soda. "You say that like it's a bad thing."

"It's a very slippery thing," I say. "But I'm not complaining."

We look at each other and burst into another fit of giggles.

"Seriously though," McKenzy says, wiping her eyes. "You've got the ultimate setup. You have a gorgeous place in one of the coolest cities on Earth, a billionaire sugar daddy who buys you apartments and flies you around the world, a sexy football player boyfriend who'll probably win MVP, and two more insanely hot boyfriends who are both wildly in love with you."

"When you put it like that, it sounds…." I pause, searching for the right word.

"Unfair?" she supplies.

"Absurd," I correct. "Like I stepped into some alternate reality where my sex life got scripted by a horny fairy godmother."

McKenzy laughs so hard she falls backward onto my pillows. "I'm not even mad. I'm just proud of you. Remember when we used to stay up all night in college, drinking boxed wine and fantasizing about future husbands? And now here you are, starring in *The Art of Having It All.*"

I groan, throwing a pillow at her. "Do not make that the title of my memoir."

"Oh, I absolutely will."

We collapse into fits of laughter again until McKenzy sits up, suddenly thoughtful. "Hey, real talk for a sec?"

"Uh-oh." I brace myself.

"You're happy, right? Like, really happy… with all of this."

I smile, and it's softer this time. "Yeah. I am."

She studies me like she's trying to read between the lines. "Even with all the… juggling?"

"It's a lot," I admit. "But I love them, all of them. And they love me. Somehow, it works."

McKenzy shakes her head in awe. "You're my hero, bitch."

I roll onto my stomach, propping my chin on my hands. "You know, Damien offered to buy me the apartment after I was freaking out about the logistics. He made it sound so casual, like *'Oh, you should have a home base in San Francisco.'* Who does that?"

"Damien Blackwood, apparently."

"It's gorgeous, too," I say dreamily. "I've only seen pictures so far, but there's a balcony overlooking the bay and a walk-in closet the size of our living room."

McKenzy whistles. "Damn."

"And he stocked the bathroom with all my favorite products, like, the expensive stuff I can only afford when Sephora has a sale."

"That man worships the ground you walk on."

"They all do."

"And you deserve it," she says firmly. "After all the crap you've been through? I'm glad you found guys who treat you right."

I feel my throat tighten, and I blink fast to keep the tears at bay. "Thanks, Kenz."

She grins and nudges me with her elbow. "Now, let's talk wardrobe. You need at least one slutty dress for post-game celebrations."

"Already packed."

"And lingerie. Duh."

I flip open my lingerie drawer and hold up a sheer red baby doll with a matching thong. "Prepared."

"God, you're good."

"And Rafe's jersey," I add, tossing it into the suitcase.

McKenzy's eyes go wide. "Oh my God, are you gonna wear it with nothing underneath?"

"Maybe."

"You're a menace."

"I learned from the best."

She bows. "Thank you, thank you."

We spend the next hour debating outfits, planning hypothetical date nights in San Francisco, and gossiping about which one of my boyfriends is most likely to cause trouble during the trip. Consensus: Damien.

By the time my suitcase is finally packed, I'm buzzing with excitement and nerves. "This is really happening," I say softly.

"It really is."

"I have to get this right."

"You will," McKenzy says confidently. "You always do."

I hug her tight. She's my best friend who's been with me through everything—from bad dates to heartbreak to kidnappings to polyamorous chaos. "Thanks for being my person."

"Always."

As she heads toward the door, she pauses. "Hey, Harper?"

"Yeah?"

"If you need me to fly to San Francisco to referee your boyfriends, I'm only a phone call away."

I laugh. "I'll keep that in mind."

When she's gone, I flop back on my bed, staring at the ceiling. Four men. One weekend. My life is wild. And I wouldn't trade a second of it.

Rafe

I didn't think I'd like San Francisco this much. Minnesota will always be home, but there's something about this place that makes me feel like I can breathe a little deeper. Maybe it's the ocean air, or the way the city hums with a different kind of energy. Or maybe it's just because this is the first time in my life where it feels like everything isn't mapped out for me in advance.

Back home, everyone knew me before I even opened my mouth–quarterback, hometown hero, the guy who lost the love of his life, then somehow got her back. But here, nobody knows my story unless I tell them. I'm just another new player trying to prove I deserve the spot they gave me.

And yeah, that's terrifying. But it's also kind of exhilarating.

The guys on the team are solid. Some of them are younger, fresh out of college with that cocky glow that only lasts until you hit your first real injury. Some are vets who've seen it all and can spot a rookie mistake from a mile away. I'm somewhere in between, not a newbie, but not a legend either. Yet.

They like me, though. I'm funny enough to chime in on the locker room jokes and good enough on the field to make them trust me when it counts. It's a delicate balance, being confident without being a dick… and, of course, hiding the fact that my love life is straight out of a soap opera.

No one's asked about Harper yet, but it's only a matter of time. I don't know how to casually mention that my girlfriend is dating three other guys and somehow we're all cool with it. It's not exactly standard locker room talk.

I'm hanging up my helmet in the locker room when my phone buzzes. Harper's name lights up the screen, and just seeing it makes me grin like an idiot.

Harper: We're on the jet! Scott just found the massage chair button, and now he's never leaving.

I laugh, shaking my head.

Me: Tell him he can keep the chair. I just want you.

She sends back a string of heart emojis and a very inappropriate GIF that makes me snort loud enough that one of my teammates glances over.

"You good?" he asks.

"Great," I say, and I mean it.

Knowing Harper's coming to my first home game feels like a lucky charm I didn't realize I needed. And even though her other lovers are also coming, and even though Damien is bankrolling the whole thing,

I don't feel threatened in the slightest. She's here for me, and I'm going to play a hell of a game to impress her.

As strange as our situation may be, I love that Harper is so open with all of us. She doesn't split herself into quarters. She loves us all with her whole self. When I'm with her, I don't have to wonder what she shares with the others, what parts of herself she doesn't give to me.

She gives me everything.

Game day dawns bright and clear, the perfect California morning shown in movies. I thought it was just Hollywood magic, but it actually is shaping out to be a perfect day. Unfortunately, my stomach is a mess, part nerves, part excitement, part knowing Harper will be here shortly. She'll be up in the stands somewhere, making a scene.

She's the loudest fan I've ever had. Even in high school, when she barely understood the rules, she screamed herself silly at every game. I picture her in the stands now, wearing my jersey and a ridiculous amount of glitter, waving a homemade sign that's half inside joke, half inappropriate.

In the locker room, the energy is palpable. Everyone's hyped. It's the first home game of the season, and this will set the tone for everything that comes after.

I tape my wrists, lace my cleats, and sit for a minute, letting the noise fade out. I think about the first time I ever held a football, back when I was five and my dad tossed one to me in the backyard. I think about Harper, how she used to sit on the sidelines with her sketchbook, pretending to take notes about the plays when she was just doodling my name. I think about all the things I almost lost and how lucky I am to have them back.

Running onto the field at the start of the game is a high nothing else can touch. The crowd roars, the sun beats down, and for a second, I'm just a kid again, playing for the love of the game.

I can't wait.

6

———

THE LAP OF LUXURY

Damien's jet is my new favorite place in the world. I mean, I love my apartment, I love everywhere I go with my guys, and I even love my tiny little Prius back home. But this is luxury wrapped in silk, dipped in champagne, and handed to me on a silver platter.

Scott is playing with the massage chair, testing every setting like a kid on Christmas morning. Tomas, ever composed, reading something on his tablet, pretending like he's not secretly enjoying the five-star treatment. And Damien? Damien is lounging like a king, sipping whiskey in a glass that was probably hand-blown in some exclusive European workshop.

"I could get used to this," I say with a sigh, stretching my legs on the reclining seat.

"You *should* get used to it," Damien says, swirling his drink. "This is your life now."

I snort. "Oh, is it? Just like that?"

"Just like that." He smirks. "I refuse to let my favorite people travel like peasants."

Scott groans, adjusting his chair. "Damien, I don't know how to tell you this, but I might never leave."

Tomas glances up from his tablet. "He's not joking."

"I know." Damien grins. "I'll have the crew prepare his room permanently."

Scott sighs dramatically. "Finally, someone who appreciates me."

I laugh, shaking my head. "You're all ridiculous."

By the time we land in San Francisco, I'm practically bouncing in my seat.

Rafe's first home game with the 49ers–one of the best teams in the NFL. And knowing I get to be here, that I get to cheer him on in person, that he'll be looking for me in the crowd, makes my heart feel full to bursting.

But before the game, Damien has another surprise waiting for me.

"I figured," he says casually, leading us to a sleek black SUV waiting outside the private terminal, "since we have a little time before the game, you should see your new home."

Scott whistles. "Here we go."

Tomas raises a brow. "That sounds ominous."

I stare at Damien with unbridled excitement. I didn't think I'd get to see it until after the game.

We pull up to the luxury building I've only seen in pictures. Damien's driver holds the door open for all of us as Damien leads us into the building with a fancy fob and up to the penthouse level. Scott lets out a low whistle the second we step inside. "Damn."

Tomas, ever the composed one, nods approvingly. "This is impresionante."

Impressive doesn't even cover it. The apartment is... I don't even have words.

The place is massive. Floor-to-ceiling windows overlook the city skyline, casting a golden glow over the sleek, modern furniture. The kitchen is straight out of a Michelin three-star restaurant. The living room has plush velvet couches that I already know I'm going to fall asleep on.

But the closet... oh, my God, the closet. It's bigger than my bedroom back home. The shelves are lined with designer handbags, shoes that scream luxury, and dresses that I know Damien picked out specifically for me.

I turn in a slow circle, blinking at the sheer excess of it all. "I can't believe how beautiful this is," I whisper.

Scott shakes his head, running a hand down a soft suede jacket hanging near the entrance. "This is unreal."

"This is insanity," I say, spinning to face Damien. "I would've been fine with a little studio. Are you sure this isn't too much?"

"Yes." He's utterly unbothered, sliding his hands into his pockets like he didn't just casually gift me a property worth millions.

"Why?"

Damien tilts his head as if he's genuinely confused. "Because you deserve only the finest things in life, and I have the means to give that to you."

I open my mouth. Close it. Open it again.

Tomas chuckles softly. "You broke her."

Scott nods. "That's fair. I'd be broken too if someone just handed me a luxury penthouse."

I press my hands to my face. "Damien, this is too much."

"It's not too much." He steps closer, his voice softer. "You deserve it."

I let out a slow breath, pulling my hands away. He's looking at me like I mean something, like this isn't about money or extravagance. It's about me.

And that's what breaks me.

I launch myself at him, arms wrapping around his neck. He chuckles, catching me with ease, hands settling at my waist.

"Thank you," I whisper into his shoulder.

"Anything for you, baby."

After a very thorough tour (and Scott loudly claiming the guest room because, quote, "If Damien bought Harper an apartment, he sure as hell bought me a spare room,") we head to the stadium.

I don't think I've ever been this excited for a football game. I've been to plenty of them, of course. I spent my entire high school career on the sidelines watching Rafe play. And, of course, I got to see him play a few times in Minnesota. Something about this one feels different, though. Maybe it's the new city, or maybe it's the feeling that Rafe and I are closer than we've ever been.

The VIP box Damien secured for us is absurd. There's a fully stocked bar, plush seating, and an actual server who's dedicated to bringing us food whenever we want.

"This," Scott says, sinking into a leather seat, "is the only way I ever want to watch sports ever again."

Tomas sips a drink. "Agreed."

I can't sit still.

When Rafe finally runs onto the field, I lose it. I scream his name, waving my arms like an absolute lunatic. I know he can't hear me, and it's doubtful he can even see me, but I swear, for a split second, he turns toward our box.

Damien leans back, smirking. "He's looking for you."

Scott laughs. "Oh, yeah. He's definitely found you"

I don't care that I'm making a scene. This is his moment, and I'm going to make damn sure he knows I'm here for all of it.

The game is electrifying. Rafe is on fire, throwing passes like he was born to do this. Every time his team scores, I scream my head off. Every time he gets tackled, I tense up so hard that Tomas actually has to pull me back down into my seat. By the time the clock runs out, the 49ers have won, and I can't stop grinning.

Rafe did it. His first home game win, and I was here to see it.

"This is perfect," I whisper, curled up against Scott's side.

He kisses the top of my head. "Yeah, babe. It really is."

I feel completely, absolutely whole. The stadium is still buzzing, the energy electric even though the game ended over an hour ago. Rafe played like an absolute god. I've never seen him so alive, so in his element.

I'm still riding that high when I step out of the VIP box, walking ahead of Scott and Tomas as we make our way toward the elevators. Damien left a few minutes ago to take a call, and I don't see him anywhere just yet. The halls are packed, reporters scurrying to get last-minute interviews, and fans lingering, soaking up the victory vibes. I feel weightless, giddy with excitement for Rafe.

Then I hear Damien's voice, low and secretive from somewhere in a corner. I don't mean to eavesdrop. Really, I don't. But he's standing a few feet away, his back turned, phone pressed to his ear, and something about his tone makes my feet pause. "Yeah," he says smoothly, voice low. "Told you they'd cover the spread. Easy money."

My stomach tilts, but I don't know why.

It's Damien. He's a businessman. Of course, he bets on everything. I mean, it makes sense, right? He has more money than God, so why shouldn't he throw some of it at sports? It's not illegal for him to gamble on games, especially since he's not the one playing.

But still, something about it nags at me. Before I can overthink it, Damien ends the call, turns, and spots me standing there. His expression doesn't change, not at first. Then, he smirks, like he knows I heard him. "You look deep in thought, little red bird."

I shake my head, forcing a casual smile. "Just waiting for the guys."

"Ah." He steps closer, brushing a thumb across my jaw in that effortless way he always does. "Rafe played well today."

"Yeah," I say, regaining my composure. "He was incredible."

"Your boy's making a name for himself," Damien murmurs, slipping his phone into his pocket. "Bet that feels good."

I hesitate for half a second before nodding. "It really does."

He studies me for a beat, something flickering behind his sharp gaze. "You're overthinking something."

"I'm not." I laugh, pushing his chest lightly. "You're imagining things."

"Mmm." He hums, unconvinced. "Come on, let's get out of here."

After the game, we head back to my apartment, something I'm going to have to get used to. Scott, Tomas, and Damien sprawl across the couches like they belong here, and I can't even argue because they do.

Damien pours champagne, Scott orders too much food, and Tomas picks a random documentary on the TV that none of us watch because we're too busy talking over it. When Rafe finally arrives,

Scott and Tomas head toward their hotel, Damien leaves for his red-eye flight, and I finally get Rafe to myself.

I don't realize how much I've missed him, really missed him, until he steps inside, and everything suddenly feels right again. He sets down his duffel bag and exhales, rolling his shoulders like he's shedding the weight of the entire game. I don't wait for him to settle. I launch myself at him, arms wrapping around his neck, my lips crashing into his before he can say a single word.

He catches me like he always does, hands firm on my waist, pulling me against him so tight I can feel his heartbeat.

"Hey," he murmurs against my mouth.

"Hey."

His fingers slide into my hair, his breath warm against my cheek. "You were loud."

I grin. "You couldn't hear me."

"Sugar, I think the entire stadium heard you." He laughs.

"Good." I press another kiss to his jaw. "You deserve to be screamed for."

His grip tightens, but his voice drops. "Thank you for being here."

"I wouldn't have missed it for anything."

His forehead rests against mine for a second, and in that small moment, I let myself breathe him in… the scent of his skin, the warmth of his body, the comfort of knowing that no matter how much distance is between us, he is still mine.

"Come here," he murmurs, pulling me toward the couch. "Let's just… be."

And so we are.

We curl up together on the ridiculously plush sectional, my legs draped over his, his arm tucked around my waist. The city hums outside, lights twinkling, but all I care about is the way he holds me, like he never wants to let go.

I don't tell him about Damien's phone call.

Right now, all that matters is this.

7

REUNITED

Rafe

Harper is here. In my city. In her own apartment. In my arms.

I don't think it's fully hit me yet. The past few weeks have been a blur—a new team, new city, new life—but now, finally, it feels like I can breathe again. She's actually here, curled up against my chest like she belongs there, like she's always belonged there. And she always has.

Her hair's a little messy from where she fell asleep on me earlier after our first round of sex, strands sticking up in every direction, and I swear I've never seen anything more perfect. She's got on one of my old sweatshirts, her bare legs tucked under her, scrolling through some takeout menu like it's the most important decision of her life.

"I'm getting you the spicy basil chicken," she announces without even looking up.

I raise a brow. "Not even gonna let me pick?"

"Nope." She grins, so bright and cheeky it should come with a warning label. "I know you too well."

She's right. She does. And I love her for it.

The food arrives faster than I want it to. Because before the doorbell rings, we are wrapped up in each other, sheets tangled, my mouth tracing every curve I'd spent weeks missing, her nails dragging down my back like she couldn't stand the space between us for another second. She's still flushed when she stands to answer the door, her thighs trembling just enough to make my chest swell with pride.

I follow her into the living room, taking a seat on the couch as she brings the food over. "You good, sugar?" I tease, arms behind my head, cocky as hell.

She tosses a napkin at my face. "Eat your damn food, Maloney."

But we both know I'm already full on her, on this night, on the way she looked at me when I opened her apartment door, and her whole face lit up like I'd just declared world peace.

The Thai food's good, but watching Harper devour dumplings like they're the only thing keeping her alive is better. She moans every time she takes a bite, the sound low and throaty, and I shift in my seat because I'm already hard again. It's not my fault. She makes everything sexual, even takeout.

"Was that your last bite?" I ask as she casually robs the final spoonful of rice right off my plate.

"Oops." She licks sauce off her thumb, absolutely unrepentant.

I shake my head, more in awe than anything. "You're lucky you're cute."

She shrugs, sitting cross-legged on the floor like a goddamn goddess who knows exactly how much power she holds over me.

"Wanna know something?" I set my chopsticks down.

"Always."

"I've missed you so much that I don't even care that you just stole my food."

She laughs, head thrown back, the kind of laugh that fills up every empty space inside me. That's the thing about Harper. Loving her has always felt like air. Necessary. Automatic. I couldn't stop if I tried.

We don't make it to the kitchen to clean up our mess. Hell, we barely make it back to the bedroom. I press her against the wall halfway down the hall, her legs wrapping around my waist like muscle memory. Her breath hitches when my fingers slide between her thighs, finding her still wet from earlier.

"Are you always this hot for me?" I ask breathlessly.

"Always," she confirms with a kiss.

I lay her down, slow and reverent, spreading her out beneath me like she's a feast I plan to consume for hours. My hands trace her body like I need to memorize her all over again. She pulls my shirt off over her head, revealing those perfect breasts. I lick a path down her stomach, tasting salt, sweat, and Harper, until I'm between her legs, tongue teasing her sensitive nub just enough to make her whimper.

"Rafe, please," she begs, already squirming.

I hold her hips still, breathing her in like a man starved. "Say it again."

"Please, Rafe." Her voice breaks just a little, and I can't resist another second. I devour her like I've dreamed of doing every night we've been apart, licking and sucking until she's gasping my name. She comes hard, fingers twisted in my hair, thighs shaking around my face, and it's the most beautiful fucking thing I've ever seen.

When I slide inside her, it's slow, almost sweet. We both know we have all night, all our lives if we want, so there's no need to rush. I watch her face as I move, every gasp and shudder, until she pulls me down, kissing me like it's been years instead of weeks. It hits me all over again. This is my girl. She always has been.

I wake up to sunlight and Harper's hair in my face. She's still draped over me, her breath warm against my chest, her leg hooked around my waist. I stroke my hand down her back, and she hums, half asleep.

"Hungry?" she murmurs.

"For food?" I grin. "Or for you?"

She groans into my skin. "You are so cocky in the morning."

"And you love it." I roll her onto her back, pinning her with my weight.

"Morning sex or cinnamon rolls?"

Her eyes sparkle. "Both." That's my invitation to take her again.

An hour later, brunch is lazy and perfect. We find a little corner café, sharing a cinnamon roll the size of my head, her foot resting on my knee under the table. She steals my bacon, and I let her. She gets whipped cream on her lip, and I wipe it away with my thumb, then suck it into my mouth while she watches with wide eyes.

"Rafe."

"What?" I grin.

"You're gonna get us arrested."

"Only if you can't behave."

I almost forget about my PT appointment until my phone buzzes. Harper pouts, but when I invite her along, her whole face lights up.

"Really? You want me there?"

"Baby, I want you everywhere."

The 49ers facility feels different with her there, like my two worlds are finally overlapping. She clings to my arm, looking around like she's on a VIP tour, and my chest swells with pride.

I introduce her to my trainer, my coach, some of the guys. No one says anything about my complicated love life because Harper just fits. Not that there haven't been a few sideways looks when I've told them we aren't exclusive. Jeff McNaught, my second-string, has definitely said a few things about it. When he meets her, he at least has the decency not to say anything rude to her face. He can be an ass, but at least he cleans up his locker room talk in her presence, though I notice his gaze lingers on her a bit. I make a mental note to have a serious talk with him later about that.

Meanwhile, Harper fits in well with the others here. She charms the equipment manager, talks shop with the trainers about injury prevention, and my teammates practically line up to meet the girl who makes me grin like a lovesick idiot.

"You've been studying," I say after she casually asks about my conditioning drills.

She shrugs, but her smile is soft. "I like knowing how to take care of you."

My heart twists in my chest. I walk her to her Uber, reluctant to let her go. She leans in, pressing her forehead to mine.

"Come visit soon?"

"Try and stop me."

I kiss her, slow and deep, right there in the parking lot where anyone can see, because fuck it. This girl has owned my heart since we were kids, and I'm done pretending otherwise.

As the car pulls away, my chest aches. Because for all the glamour of the NFL, for all the dreams I've chased my whole life, none of it feels quite right unless Harper's there to see it with me.

Harper

The plane hums softly beneath me, a low, steady vibration that lulls me into sleep almost the second I buckle my seatbelt. It has been a long, incredible, exhausting weekend, and the moment my head rests against the plush first-class seat, I'm out.

At some point, I stir slightly when Scott nudges me, pressing a warm cup of tea into my hands before I can even open my eyes. I sip it drowsily, mumbling a thank you, but the warmth only pulls me deeper into sleep. I hear the faint murmur of Scott and Tomas talking beside me, the occasional chuckle as they recap the trip, but it all feels far away.

By the time the plane touches down in St. Paul, I have to blink myself back into consciousness. The familiar, crisp Minnesota air seeps into the cabin as the doors open, and I stretch with a sigh, trying to shake off the grogginess.

McKenzy is waiting for us at baggage claim, practically bouncing on the balls of her feet when she spots us. She wears her usual leggings and oversized hoodie, her brown curls in a messy bun on top of her head. The second I see her, I grin.

"Oh, my God," she shrieks, running toward us with her arms spread wide. "There they are! My jet-setting, football-loving, ridiculously attractive trio!"

I laugh as she throws herself at me first, hugging me like I've been gone for months instead of a few days. "I take it you missed me?"

"Missed you?" she scoffs. "I lived vicariously through you! You know how many times I refreshed my phone waiting for updates?"

She pulls back and turns to Scott next, giving him a much more reasonable hug.

"So," she asks, wiggling her brows. "How was the trip? How was the game?"

Scott grins, running a hand through his hair as we all start toward the exit. "What happens in San Francisco stays in San Francisco."

McKenzy gasps dramatically. "Oh, my god. You did something scandalous, didn't you?"

Scott laughs, shaking his head. "Relax, drama queen. I had a couple of drinks at the hotel bar, ate way too much room service on Damien's tab, and went to bed early."

McKenzy huffs in disappointment. "Well, that's boring."

Scott grins wider. "But the game was amazing. Best one I've ever been to."

She turns to Tomas, who has been smiling quietly through the exchange. "What about you, professor? Anything scandalous?"

Tomas smirks, adjusting the strap of his overnight bag on his shoulder. "Not unless you consider visiting family scandalous. I met up with my cousins at an old dive bar, had a few drinks, and got to see my aunt and uncle before I flew home."

McKenzy sighs. "God, you all had the most wholesome trip ever, didn't you?"

I nudge her. "You wanted us to do something illegal?"

"A little drama would've been nice," she admits with a shrug. "Maybe one of you getting kicked out of the stadium for fighting a referee? I don't know. Give me something."

Scott chuckles. "Sorry to disappoint."

As we reach McKenzy's car, a warmth settles in my chest. As amazing as the trip has been, it is nice to be home.

After dropping Scott and Tomas off at their respective places, McKenzy and I drive toward our apartment. The city lights blur past the window, and I lean my head against the glass, lost in thought.

McKenzy must have noticed, because she nudges my arm.

"Alright, spill. You've been quiet since we left the airport. What's going on in that chaotic brain of yours?"

I chew my lip before glancing at her. "Did I tell you about Rafe's second-string quarterback?"

She raises an eyebrow. "No, but I'm intrigued. Go on."

"Well, when Rafe introduced me to some of his teammates, there was one guy, Jeff McNaught, who was… I don't know. Weird."

"Weird how?"

I hesitate. "I might be imagining it, but it felt like he was either glaring at me or undressing me with his eyes. And I can't figure out which."

McKenzy sucks in a breath. "Yikes. Creeper vibes?"

I shrug. "Maybe? Or maybe he's just pissed that Rafe's the starting QB now instead of him. I mean, I get it, he lost his position when they brought Rafe in."

"That's true." McKenzy taps her fingers against the wheel. "But also, what if he's just obsessed with you?"

I groan. "Please don't put that into the universe."

"I mean, come on," she teases. "Hotshot quarterback? Broody and resentful? Eyeing the sexy artist girlfriend of the guy who took his spot? This is prime villain origin story material."

I snort. "You watch too many crime documentaries."

"I'm just saying." She glances over at me. "Was he cute?"

I blink. "What?" I ask, incredulously.

She smirks. "Was he hot? Are you gonna add a fifth boyfriend?"

I smack her arm. "Oh, my God, McKenzy."

She cackles, dodging my retaliation. "I'm just checking!"

I shake my head, laughing despite myself. "For the record? No. He was not hot. And even if he was, I think I'm at my max capacity for boyfriends."

McKenzy sighs dramatically. "Fine. But if you change your mind, let me know. I'm emotionally invested in your harem."

I roll my eyes, but my stomach still twists just a little. Because even though I was joking about Jeff McNaught being a problem, something about the way he looked at me hadn't felt harmless.

By the time we get home, I am exhausted. I barely have the energy to kick off my shoes before collapsing face-first onto my bed.

The last thing I hear before sleep takes me is McKenzy calling from the other room, "Don't worry, I'll make coffee when you wake up!"

A couple of hours later, I blink awake to the smell of fresh coffee.

McKenzy is in the kitchen, already on her second cup, scrolling on her phone when I stumble in.

"I let you sleep," she says. "Aren't I the best roommate ever?"

"The best," I murmur, grabbing a mug and taking a sip.

She glances at me over the rim of her cup. "So, what's the plan now? Back to painting masterpieces?"

I hesitate, looking around our small but very full apartment. "Actually, I wanted to talk to you about that."

McKenzy raises an eyebrow. "Oh?"

"I think we should rent a studio space together," I say. "Your furniture projects are taking over, and I need more room to paint. I think it's time."

She stares at me for a second, then slams her cup on the counter. "YES."

I laugh. "That was an enthusiastic yes."

"Are you kidding?" she gasps. "I've been waiting for you to suggest this! Let's do it. Tomorrow."

8

NOTHING TOO EXTRAVAGANT

Harper

The apartment in Minnesota is quiet except for the rhythmic strokes of my brush against the canvas. There's a kind of peace in painting, something about the way colors blend together, the way shapes emerge from nothing, the way my hands move without me having to think. It's one of the few things in my life that feels truly simple.

Except today, my mind refuses to be quiet. I keep thinking about Scott and his stronger-than-expected feelings, and the fact that I can't stop thinking about him.

I dip my brush into the deep crimson paint, swirling it onto the canvas with long, sweeping strokes. I tell myself I'm just painting shadows, but I know the truth. I'm painting Scott's lips, the color they turn when he kisses me, when he really kisses me.

I press my lips together, remembering the way he looked at me at the carnival. The way he held my hand. The way he invited me to a family event without hesitation, like I already belonged.

And that's the thing, isn't it? Scott seems to be falling in love with me. He seems to see a future with me.

And I have no idea what to do with that.

I try to brush the thought away, both literally and figuratively, swiping more paint onto the canvas, but it doesn't leave. It's not that Scott has ever tried to change me. He has never once suggested I choose him over anyone else. He doesn't get jealous, doesn't demand anything.

But Scott is the kind of man who settles down.

He's the kind of man who wants a wife, a home, a family with a picket fence. He's stable, grounded in a way that makes my heart ache. And I wonder, maybe for the first time, what happens if he wakes up one day and realizes that I'll never be that for him.

Would I be able to let go of Damien? Rafe? Tomas? Would I ever want to?

I put the brush down, letting out a deep breath.

"No," I whisper to myself. "Don't go there."

It's stupid to think that far ahead. What the two of us have is good. I need to enjoy it instead of overanalyzing it.

I'm still staring at my half-finished painting when my phone buzzes. I pick it up, rolling my eyes at the name flashing across the screen.

Damien.

Because of course.

I answer. "Tell me you're not about to send me another absurdly expensive gift."

"Too late." Damien's voice purrs through the speaker. "And I have an offer."

I raise an eyebrow. "Go on."

"There's a small get-together tonight. Nothing too extravagant."

I snort. "Damien, you consider a charity gala in Monaco a 'small get-together.'"

He chuckles, the kind of laugh that always gets me in trouble. "Trust me, you won't want to miss this. I'll pick you up at nine."

Before I can even answer, McKenzy bursts into the room with a package in her hands.

"You know–" I sigh dramatically into the phone, "you could wait for me to say yes before sending the dress."

McKenzy and I exchange looks before bursting into laughter.

Damien hums in amusement. "It's almost like I know you, little red bird."

I shake my head, already smiling. "Fine. I'll see you at nine."

"Wear the dress," he says smoothly before hanging up.

McKenzy throws herself onto my bed, already ripping open the package. She gasps dramatically as she pulls the gown from the box. "Harper. Oh, my God."

I step closer, letting out a small breathless laugh as I take it in. It's exotic, sleek, black silk with intricate beading, the kind of dress that makes a woman look like she owns the world just by wearing it.

McKenzy waves a hand at the gown. "You know, Damien may be a controlling billionaire, but at least he has taste."

DAMIEN

AS HARPER STEPS OUT OF HER BUILDING, MY BREATH CATCHES. HER dress clings in all the right places, the beading catching the light in a way that makes her look almost otherworldly. Her hair falls in loose waves, her lips painted the perfect shade of red, dark, dangerous… a promise.

I should have expected this. She always has a way of surpassing expectations, but even after all this time, she still manages to leave me speechless. She smirks as she slides into the car, raising a brow at my utter lack of words.

"What?" she teases. "Have I finally managed to impress you, Mr. Blackwood?"

I let out a slow breath, composing myself, even though every cell in my body is telling me to take her upstairs instead of to this damn party.

"Little red bird," I murmur, taking her hand and bringing it to my lips. "You don't impress me."

Her brow furrows, but before she can argue, I kiss the inside of her wrist, watching her shiver at the contact. "You destroy me."

Her breath hitches. Good. That makes two of us.

The car moves smoothly through the city, the skyline fading behind us as we drive toward the outskirts. I know Harper isn't worried. She trusts me, even if she doesn't always admit it. But she's curious, and her fingers fidget with the edge of her dress, her gaze flickering between me and the window as the lights of the city turn into empty stretches of road.

"Okay," she finally says, crossing one leg over the other. "I give in. Where the hell are we going?"

I smirk. "Impatient?"

She narrows her eyes. "You literally refuse to tell me anything in advance. This could be a murder mystery party, Damien."

"Would you still come with me if it was?"

She considers it. "Depends. Am I the victim or the murderer?"

I chuckle, shaking my head. "Neither."

"Then what?"

I glance out the window as the trees get thicker, the road darker. "It's a private gathering."

Harper hums. "That tells me nothing."

I exhale, feigning dramatic exhaustion. "Have you ever been this far out into the wilderness before?"

She snorts. "Damien, we're in Minnesota. This is not the wilderness."

I tilt my head. "We're at least forty minutes outside the city. No streetlights. No neighbors. Miles of land between us and anyone else."

Her smirk falters just a little. "You're making it sound a lot creepier than it probably is."

"Am I?" I tease, leaning in slightly.

She swats at my arm. "Just tell me where we're going."

I chuckle, but before I can answer, the car slows, pulling onto a long, winding driveway. At the end is a mansion straight out of a gothic novel. The house looms ahead of us, massive and dramatic with Victorian architecture, deep ebony woodwork, and tall windows that flicker with golden light from within.

Harper leans forward, pressing a hand to the window. "Okay, this is a murder mystery house."

I laugh, placing a hand on her knee. "No murder. Just art."

She glances at me, eyes gleaming. "Art?"

"You'll see."

The car rolls to a stop in front of the grand entrance, and before she can press me further, the driver steps out to open her door. Harper hesitates for half a second, taking in the sheer intimidating beauty of the house.

And I can't wait to show her exactly what awaits inside.

HARPER

THE MANSION LOOKS LIKE A DREAM. EVEN IN THE DARK OF THE NIGHT, the full moon's glow is enough to highlight its intricate details. The exterior is deep ebony, sleek and rich like ink poured against the sky. Lavender trim winds its way around the windows, curling like delicate vines, making the entire structure look like it belongs in a Tim Burton movie.

I stand at the base of the winding sidewalk, staring up at it, completely entranced.

"This is gorgeous." I breathe, my fingers tightening around Damien's arm. "Where are we? What is this place?"

"Just a place where starving artists hang out," he replies smoothly, winking as he guides me forward.

I giggle, shaking my head. "Of course it is," I respond sarcastically.

The moment we step inside, I realize Damien has, once again, undersold things dramatically.

This isn't just a party. This isn't just a gathering of creatives. This is a full-fledged artist's soirée, the kind of thing you read about in memoirs of brilliant and tragic geniuses who shaped the world with their work.

The ballroom is vast, stretching out before me in a whirlwind of golden light, deep mahogany floors, and velvet drapery. The ceiling towers above us, adorned with a breathtaking fresco that reminds me of the Sistine Chapel, but with more rebellion, more chaos.

The space is alive. People are standing in clusters, deep in discussion, their hands moving animatedly as they talk about topics I can't quite catch. Some are drinking, some are dancing, some are making out against intricately carved columns like they're in a French novel.

And oh, my God, the art–it's everywhere. The walls are lined with pieces that shouldn't exist in the same room together. Classical masterpieces sit alongside modern experimental pieces, sculptures that look like they could breathe, sketches so raw they practically weep.

This is the kind of place people write about years later, reminiscing about the time they met someone who changed their life forever.

I blink, trying to take it all in, trying to process how the hell I ended up here. And then, as if to prove that I really do live in a fantasy novel, I spot him–Michael Vernon, my favorite artist of all time.

"Damien," I whisper, gripping his arm so hard he actually winces. "Is that Michael Vernon?"

Damien smirks. "Yes. And he's coming this way."

Oh, God.

I try to compose myself, reminding myself that we've met once before. Meeting your hero even a second time isn't that easy, though.

"Blackwood," he says, clapping Damien on the shoulder.

"Vernon," Damien replies, just as smoothly. "You remember Harper Ward?"

Michael Vernon turns to me, his piercing green eyes studying me like I'm something worth painting. "Of course, Harper," he muses. "I've been watching your work."

I forget how to breathe. "You," my voice dies in my throat. "You've seen my work?"

I think I've ascended to another plane of existence. Damien chuckles beside me, clearly enjoying my reaction. "Harper was just telling me she's thinking of renting a studio space."

Michael perks up. "Good. You need one."

I blink. "You think so?"

"Absolutely." He gestures around us. "An artist needs a space that belongs only to them. Where you create should be separate from where you sleep. Otherwise, you'll never know where the art ends and you begin."

That thought lingers in my mind, settling in deep. Because he's right. I've always painted in my apartment, shoving canvases into whatever corner would hold them. But maybe I do need something more.

Michael clasps my shoulder before stepping away. "I look forward to seeing what you create next." And just like that, he's gone, disappearing into the sea of people.

I turn to Damien, still reeling. "Did that just happen?"

The rest of the night is a blur of champagne, whispered conversations, and moments I'll never forget. Damien is the perfect escort, never letting me feel out of place, always introducing me to people who inspire me. I meet painters, sculptors, filmmakers, writers—people who have shaped the art world in ways I can only hope to one day achieve.

By the time the party starts to wind down, I feel changed, like something inside me has shifted, like I've been given a glimpse into the future I've always wanted, and now I just have to reach out and take it.

The ride back to Damien's penthouse is quiet, but it's the kind of silence that means something.

I stare out the window, watching the city lights blur past, still lost in the night.

Damien's watching me, I can feel it, but he doesn't say anything. He doesn't need to. We both know exactly how this night will end.

The next morning, I wake up wrapped in expensive sheets, the lingering taste of champagne and Damien still on my lips.

The night was magic. And I can't wait to tell McKenzy everything.

I roll over, stretching, but Damien's not beside me. Instead, there's a note on the pillow.

"Had to handle business. My driver will take you home whenever you're ready. Can't wait to see you again."

I smile, running my fingers over the ink.

When I get home, McKenzy is waiting like a vulture. "Tell me everything."

And so, I do.

9

———

THE WOMAN SCORNED

When Tomas calls a few days later and asks if I want to go salsa dancing at our usual spot, I smile so wide my face hurts.

"Of course," I say, already flipping through my closet for a dress that will make him sweat before we even hit the dance floor. "I'm dying for another night with you, Profe."

When Tomas knocks on my door, I'm already feeling dangerous.

The dress I picked is deep green, tight in all the right places, with a slit high enough to make a statement. My heels click against the floor as I open the door, and the moment Tomas lays eyes on me, his whole body goes still.

His gaze travels down my body, slow and deliberate, before snapping back to my face with a heated intensity that sends a shiver down my spine.

"Helena," he breathes, shaking his head as he steps inside. "You are . . . *imposible*."

I grin, letting my fingers trail along his chest before resting on his shoulder. "Impossible to resist?"

"Completely." He finds my waist, pulling me closer. "Let's get to the club before I forget to do the resisting."

At the club, when the music starts, my body moves with his without thinking. Tomas leads, and I follow. His hands guide me through spins and dips, my heels clicking perfectly to the beat, my dress flaring around my legs as I move. I feel free. Salsa is sexy, intoxicating, and the way Tomas's hands skim my waist, the way his breath ghosts my ear as we move, makes the entire dance feel like foreplay.

He feels it, too. I can tell. Every time our bodies brush together, his grip tightens, his eyes darken, and his movements grow hungrier. He spins me once, then again, before dipping me so low I can feel his breath against my neck. I shiver.

"Helena," he murmurs, his voice rough. "You're going to drive me insane."

"That's the plan," I whisper back, grinning as he pulls me upright.

After two dances, I need a break. "I'm going to freshen up," I tell him, pressing a quick kiss to his cheek before weaving my way toward the ladies' room.

The hallway is dimmer, quieter, and as I walk, I let my fingers trail along the smooth wall, still feeling the lingering thrill of the dance floor. But then, without warning, something shifts.

The air feels thicker, charged with something I can't quite name. The hairs on the back of my neck stand up. And then I hear a sharp click of heels behind me. I turn, and my stomach drops.

Tomas's ex-wife, Carmen, stands just a few feet away, arms crossed, her sharp eyes locked directly on me. She's stunning. She's tall, sleek, and intimidating in a way that's not just about looks.

And she looks like she might murder me.

I straighten my spine, plastering a polite expression on my face. "Carmen."

She steps closer, her lips curling into something that isn't quite a smile. "So," she says, her voice smooth but laced with venom, "Tomas is still wasting his time with you."

My heart beats faster, but I keep my face calm. "Wasting?" I ask, tilting my head. "Funny, he seems to think otherwise."

Her eyes flash. "Listen to me, *puta*," she hisses, stepping even closer. "Stay the hell away from him."

My stomach tightens, but I refuse to back down. "You don't get to tell me what to do."

Carmen laughs, but there's no humor in it. "You really think you matter?" She leans in, her breath hot against my skin. "You're just a distraction, a blip in time. Tomas belongs to me."

I clench my jaw. "I don't think he got that memo."

Her smile vanishes, replaced with pure rage.

I step back, ready to walk away, but she suddenly switches to Spanish, her words rapid and seething. *"Si te vuelvo a ver con él, te juro que te mataré."*

If I see you with him again, I swear I'll kill you.

Ice trickles down my spine.

Her face is too close, her expression too sharp, and every instinct in my body screams at me to leave. I turn and bolt. I practically slam into Tomas when I reach the edge of the dance floor.

He catches me immediately, hands steady on my waist, brows furrowed.

"Helena? *Todo está bien?*"

Is everything all right?

No, everything is definitely not bien.

I look up at him, breathless, heart pounding. "Your ex-wife just threatened to kill me," I manage to say, my fingers digging into his arm.

His face darkens instantly. Something dangerous flickers in his eyes.

TOMAS

THE MOMENT I SAW HARPER RUNNING TOWARD ME, I KNEW SOMETHING was wrong.

Her face was pale, her breath coming in shallow gasps, her eyes wide with fear. I barely had time to react before she threw herself into my arms, her entire body trembling against mine.

Carmen was always jealous, always possessive, but this is insanity.

I take a deep breath, forcing myself to stay calm for Harper's sake. I can feel the unsteady rhythm of her heart against my chest, the way she's still shaking slightly, and it makes me want to find Carmen right now and end this once and for all. Instead, I hold Harper closer, pressing a kiss to the top of her head.

"She won't touch you," I promise. "She won't come near you again."

Harper lets out a slow breath, her fingers loosening against my shirt. "I know you will do everything you can to make that come true," she whispers. "But she looked so serious, Tomas. She wasn't just being dramatic. She thinks that you're her property or something, and I'm just getting in her way."

I grit my teeth, scanning the room. I half-expect to see Carmen lurking in the shadows, her dark eyes burning holes into the back of Harper's head, but she's nowhere in sight. I want to find her, to tell her to stay the hell away, to make it clear that this behavior isn't just unacceptable but dangerous. I could slap a restraining order on her right now for doing this.

But for the moment, the only thing that matters is Harper and keeping her safe. With everything she went through with her ex, the last thing she needs is Carmen La Loca coming after her.

I brush my fingers against her cheek. "Let's get you home."

She nods, exhaling slowly, and I keep my arm around her as we head for the exit.

Carmen may have gotten away tonight, but this petty drama has to end now.

❧

HARPER

. . .

TOMAS'S HAND IS WARM IN MINE, HIS THUMB BRUSHING SOFTLY OVER MY knuckles as we sit in the car, parked outside my building. Neither of us speaks for a moment, the weight of what just happened hanging heavy between us.

"I'm so sorry, Helena," Tomas says quietly. His voice is thick with guilt, and when I glance at him, his brow is furrowed deep, his jaw tight.

"Profe." I squeeze his hand. "You have nothing to apologize for."

"But I do." He looks at me, dark eyes full of regret. "I knew Carmen was jealous. I knew she wasn't handling the divorce well. But this?" He shakes his head. "I never thought she would threaten you like that."

"I'm okay," I reassure him. "A little shaken up, but physically fine."

"That's not the point." His hand tightens slightly around mine. "She shouldn't get to ruin our night."

"She didn't." I smile softly. "I still had a perfect night with you."

His smile is faint, but it's there, and I lean over, brushing my lips to his. "Come upstairs," I whisper against his mouth. "Spend the night with me."

"Helena." He sighs my name like it's a prayer. "You deserve better than this."

"I deserve you," I counter. "Now, come inside."

Tomas follows me into my apartment, his hand never leaving mine. The moment the door shuts, he pulls me into his arms, his lips finding my forehead first, then my temple, then the corner of my mouth. It's not a hungry kiss, not yet. It's an apology wrapped in tenderness, a quiet way of saying, *I'm here, I've got you.*

"*Te adoro,*" he whispers, his fingers tracing slow patterns up and down my back. "*Desde el primer día.*" *I adore you. Since the first day.*

I press my face into his chest, breathing him in, letting his warmth soak into me. "Show me."

He pulls back, just enough to cup my face in both hands, his thumbs brushing over my cheeks. "Show you?"

"Show me how much you adore me." My voice is soft, but my meaning is crystal clear.

His eyes darken, that familiar heat flaring to life between us. "Mi preciosa."

We barely make it to my bedroom. His mouth finds mine again, this time deeper, hungrier, his hands sliding down to cup my ass and pull me flush against him. I can already feel how hard he is, and my body responds instantly, heat pooling low in my belly.

He walks me backward, his lips never leaving mine, until my knees hit the edge of the bed. I sink down, tugging him with me, my hands working at the buttons of his shirt. He shrugs it off, and I let my fingers wander over warm skin and firm muscle, tracing the faint scar along his side that I know he got trying to fix a stubborn window years ago.

"Helena," he murmurs, his lips trailing down my neck. "You're the most beautiful woman I've ever seen."

I smile, tugging his belt free. "Less talking, Profe. More touching."

He laughs softly, but the sound fades as I push his pants and boxers down, freeing his already hard cock. I wrap my hand around him, stroking slowly, loving the way his breath catches, the way his hips rock into my grip like he can't help himself.

He pulls my dress over my head, pausing just long enough to admire me, the way my nipples harden in the cool air, the way my skin flushes under his gaze.

"No bra?" he teases, brushing his thumb over my nipple.

"Didn't need one," I reply breathlessly. "I knew you'd take care of them."

"Damn right." His mouth replaces his thumb, tongue swirling, teeth grazing, while his hand slides down my stomach, into my panties. "So wet, mi preciosa," he murmurs against my skin. "All for me?"

"All for you, Profe."

He pushes my panties down, and I kick them off without a second thought. He settles between my thighs, his dark hair brushing my stomach as his mouth finds me. His tongue is slow and deliberate, his fingers spreading me open, his stubble a delicious scrape against my inner thighs.

I grip the sheets, my hips lifting to meet his mouth. "Tomas…."

"Shh, mi amor." He flicks his tongue just right, and I cry out, my whole body arching. "Let me take care of you."

He works me like a man on a mission, lapping, sucking, teasing, until I'm trembling on the edge. And then, when I'm right there, teetering, he slides two fingers inside me, angling them to press against that perfect spot. I fall apart with his name on my lips, my whole body shuddering as pleasure crashes over me. He stays between my legs, coaxing me through it, until I'm panting and pliant beneath him. "Profe," I whisper, reaching for him. "Please."

"Please what, mi preciosa?" He kisses his way back up my body, his cock brushing against my thigh.

"Please fuck me."

His groan is low and rough, and then he's sliding inside me, slow and careful, stretching me inch by inch. No matter how many times we do this, it always feels like the first time, like my body has to remember how to take all of him.

He whispers, "So fucking perfect." He starts to move, slow and deep, his forehead pressed to mine, his hands cupping my hips to guide me. "You feel like heaven, Helena."

I cling to him, my nails dragging down his back, my legs wrapping around his waist to pull him deeper. "More."

He gives me more. Faster. Rougher. His control slips, and I love it when Tomas loses control. It's like watching a gentle storm finally break loose. His hand slides between us, his thumb finding my clit, and it's enough to push me over again, my body clenching tight around his thick cock.

"Fuck," he groans. "That's it, mi amor. Give it to me."

He thrusts deep once, twice more, then follows me over the edge, his body shuddering, his breath ragged. We collapse together, his weight comforting against me, his heart pounding beneath my palm.

"I adore you," he whispers into my hair.

I smile, my fingers tracing lazy circles on his back. "Me, too, Profe."

We drift off tangled together, his body still partially inside mine, his breath warm on my skin.

64

10

———

GRANDMA'S 100TH

Scott is sprawled on my couch, scrolling through his phone, looking completely relaxed.

At least, he is until he looks up. The second I step out of my room, his phone drops onto his lap, his lips parting slightly as his eyes trail over me.

The white sundress with pink flowers had been an impulse pick– sweet, flirty, innocent enough for a family party, but still tight in all the right places. My hair is curled, cascading over my shoulders, and my perfume smells like fresh strawberries and summer dreams.

I barely make it two steps into the living room before Scott lets out a low, audible gasp.

"Oh, no," I tease, placing a hand on my hip. "Did I break you?"

He blinks once, then twice, before clearing his throat. "You're… I mean–" He stumbles, trying to gather his thoughts.

I bite back a smile. "You mean?"

Scott shakes his head, standing up slowly. "I mean I'm going to need a minute to remember my own name."

Laughing, I step forward, running a finger lightly down the front of his shirt. "Come on," I command. "We have a party to get to."

65

Scott doesn't budge. "Are you sure?"

I nod, stepping past him to grab my purse. "Yes. Your great-grandmother turns one hundred today. We are going to celebrate her."

Scott brushes my hip as I pass. "But we could celebrate here," he suggests with a wicked smirk.

I spin around, narrowing my eyes playfully. "Scott Bauer. Did you just suggest skipping your family's party because you want to jump my bones?"

His grin is shameless. "Yes."

I swat his arm. "You're impossible."

He sighs dramatically as he grabs his keys. "Fine. But for the record? I will not be thinking about anything but you for this entire party."

I loop my arm through his. "Well, if you're a good boy, maybe later I'll make whatever you were dreaming about come true."

His fingers tighten around my waist as he groans. "You're killing me, Harper."

"Drive fast," I say with a wink.

We get to the party, and I finally meet the woman of the hour. Scott's great-grandmother is a queen. The woman is tiny but fierce, dressed in an elegant blue dress, wearing pearls and bold red lipstick. She doesn't look a day over eighty, and from the way she commands the room, I'm half-convinced she's immortal.

"She's amazing," I whisper to Scott as we watch her hold court from the center of the room.

Scott grins. "She once hit my grandpa with a rolling pin because he disrespected her apple pie."

I snort. "A woman after my own heart."

The party is wonderful, filled with laughter, good food, and a warmth that wraps around me like a blanket. Scott introduces me to what feels like every single Bauer family member in existence, and I quickly realize they already know all about me. I must have made one hell of an impression at his cousin's wedding.

"Oh, so this is the famous Harper," one of his cousins I haven't met says, nudging Scott playfully. "He doesn't shut up about you."

Scott coughs loudly, shooting his cousin a look of betrayal.

I grin. "Oh? What does he say?"

Scott glares at his cousin, who turns back to me, rubbing the back of his neck. "That you're amazing."

His mother steps in, beaming at me. "It's so nice to see you again, Harper," she tells me warmly with a hug. "You make him very, very happy."

Scott groans. "Okay, we're leaving now."

After a few more well wishes to his great-grandmother, we head out the door. I'm still laughing as we get into Scott's truck, the warmth of the party lingering in my chest.

"You're so dramatic," I tease, buckling my seatbelt.

He shakes his head, starting the engine. The truck rumbles down the road, the hum of the engine filling the quiet space between us. After a few minutes, the excitement of the party wears off, and I'm suddenly weighed down again by my encounter with Carmen the other night. I sigh heavily.

"I should probably tell you something."

Scott frowns slightly. "What's up?"

I shift in my seat, turning toward him. "Tomas' ex-wife, Carmen, confronted me at the salsa club the other night."

His entire body goes rigid. "What?"

"She was waiting for me," I explain. "She cornered me in the hallway near the restroom, and she wasn't exactly friendly."

His hands tighten around the wheel. "What do you mean by 'not exactly friendly'?"

I exhale, watching the streetlights flash by. "She told me to stay away from Tomas. And then she said if she saw us together again, she'd kill me."

Scott slams the brakes at a stop sign, his jaw clenched so tightly I think it might snap. "She threatened you?"

I shrug. "It was probably just dramatic nonsense. Nothing to worry about."

He shakes his head, jaw flexing. "It doesn't matter. No one gets to threaten you, Harper."

I reach over, covering his hand with mine. "I can handle it. This is nothing like Jack."

He doesn't look convinced. After a long pause, he exhales, rubbing a hand down his face. "Do you know how to fight?"

I blink. "What?"

"If someone attacked you, would you know how to fight back?"

I scoff. "You mean, like, punch someone?"

"Yes."

I laugh. "No, not really."

Scott nods firmly, pulling into his driveway. "Then I'm going to teach you."

Once we're settled in his house, Scott clears the coffee table out of the way, rolling his shoulders back as he steps in front of me.

"All right," he says. "Lesson one, if someone is trying to hurt you, you don't hesitate. Got it?"

I cross my arms. "Got it."

He gestures toward me. "Okay. Hit me."

I blink. "What?"

He gestures again. "Hit me."

I raise an eyebrow. "You're joking, right?"

Scott grins. "Nope."

I huff, rolling my eyes. "Fine." I pull my arm back and half-heartedly tap his shoulder with my fist.

He stares at me. "Harper."

"What?"

He pinches the bridge of his nose. "I said hit me."

I shrug. "I did."

He groans. "Okay, new plan. I'll show you the moves, and then we'll practice."

I nod. "That sounds more my speed."

Scott teaches me how to palm strike, a quick, effective move aimed at the chin or nose.

Then he shows me how to elbow strike, how to knee an attacker in the stomach, and even how to kick them where it really hurts. By the time we're finished, I'm breathless and laughing, wiping sweat from my brow.

Scott shakes his head, chuckling. "I don't know if you'll ever use these, but at least you know now."

I grin. "If I ever have to palm strike someone in the face, I'll dedicate it to you."

He laughs, tugging me against his chest. "I'd expect nothing less."

SCOTT

HARPER IS ADORABLE WHEN SHE'S TRYING TO FIGHT.

She's quick, I'll give her that. She picks up on the moves faster than I expected, mirroring my stance, following my instructions with that same determined expression she gets when she's painting. She's also smart, sharp enough to anticipate what I'll tell her next before I even say it.

But she's so damn soft.

Every time she throws a punch or lands a kick, she bites her lip like she's worried about hurting me, like she's going to apologize any second. And that just kills me. Harper is just too sweet for this. She's too gentle, too demure, too her to ever want to palm-strike someone in the face.

But I want her to know how to protect herself, especially after what happened with her ex a few months ago. Still, I can't even picture her actually trying to hurt someone.

And that's why I have to be the one to keep her safe.

"Like this?" Harper asks, her brows drawn in concentration as she raises her hands into a proper defensive stance.

She's still in that damn sundress, the one that's been driving me insane since she first walked into the living room. It's white, soft, covered in tiny pink flowers, flowing just enough that every time she moves, I get a glimpse of her thighs.

It's been torture, watching her prance around in it all day, knowing I couldn't do anything about it at the party. Then I made the stupid offer to teach her self-defense, further prolonging my suffering. Now, she's standing there, looking up at me with those big, bright eyes, completely unaware of what she's doing to me.

I exhale slowly, forcing myself to focus. "Yeah, that's good. But keep your weight balanced. You want to be ready to move, not stuck in one spot."

Harper nods, adjusting her stance.

"Now, try to block me," I say, stepping forward slowly, raising my hands like I'm going to push against her shoulders.

She moves quickly, dodging to the side, her body graceful in a way that makes me forget we're supposed to be serious right now, and suddenly, I'm not thinking about fighting anymore. I'm thinking about how fucking good she looks, standing there, flushed and breathless, her chest rising and falling, that damn sundress swaying around her legs. I want to throw her over my shoulder and take her straight to bed.

Harper must see the shift in my expression because her lips part slightly, her playfulness fading into something else entirely. Something darker. Something hotter.

I step forward, closing the distance between us. "You done learning?"

She nods slowly, her breath catching.

I lift a hand, tracing my fingers over the strap of her dress. "Good."

She barely has time to react before I tug the strap down her shoulder, my mouth following its path, leaving a trail of kisses down her sun-warmed skin. Her head tilts back, a soft sigh escaping her lips as I press her gently against the wall.

"You're gorgeous when you fight," I whisper, my hand sliding down to her hip. "But you're fucking irresistible when you surrender."

Harper exhales a shaky laugh. "I thought you were teaching me to fight back."

"I am." I grip her wrist, raising her arm above her head, pinning her lightly against the wall. "But you and I both know you like it when I win."

Her pupils darken, her lips parting just slightly. "Cocky."

"Honest," I counter.

Before she can argue, I kiss her, slow at first, just the soft press of lips against lips. But it doesn't stay soft. It never does with us. Her hands slide up my chest, fingers twisting into my shirt, pulling me closer until there's not a sliver of space between us.

"On the floor," I murmur against her mouth. "Now."

Her breath stutters, but she obeys, sinking down onto the soft rug, her dress riding up her thighs as she settles back on her elbows. I kneel between her legs, sliding my hands up her calves, her thighs, pushing the fabric higher with every inch.

"Goddamn," I whisper. "You're so fucking perfect."

"Show me," she whispers back, her voice low and breathless.

I hook my fingers into her panties and pull them down her legs, tossing them somewhere behind me. She's already wet, glistening in the soft light, and my mouth waters at the sight.

I lean down, kissing her inner thigh, then the other, before my tongue finds her sweet little clit. She gasps, her hips jerking up toward me, and I grip her thighs to hold her still.

"Scott," she moans, her fingers diving into my hair.

"That's my girl," I murmur between licks, my tongue working her in slow, teasing circles. "You taste so good, sugar."

I slide a finger inside her, then two, twisting them to press against the spot that always makes her lose her mind. Sure enough, her whole body tightens, her back arching off the floor, her moans echoing through the room. She comes hard, trembling against my mouth, and I don't stop until her thighs shake, and she's begging me to kiss her.

I crawl back up her body, licking my fingers clean as I go, and her eyes go dark with hunger. "I need you," she whispers. "Right now."

"Then take me," I say, tugging down my jeans just enough to free my cock.

She wraps her legs around my waist, guiding me inside, and the second I'm fully seated, my head drops to her shoulder, a guttural groan ripping from my throat. "Oh God, baby. You feel so fucking good."

Her nails rake down my back, her hips rocking up to meet every thrust, and it's messy and desperate and perfect, our bodies colliding like they've missed each other just as much as we have.

"Harder," she begs.

And who am I to deny her?

I pin her wrists to the floor, holding her down as I fuck her deep and hard, until her cries turn into incoherent babbling, and I'm right there with her, tumbling over the edge, filling her up with everything I've got.

We collapse in a heap, both of us panting, her body still trembling around me. I kiss her softly this time, brushing her hair back from her face.

The next morning, after a few more "lessons," we sit at the table, eating in comfortable silence for a few minutes before I clear my throat. "So," I say, setting down my coffee. "How do you feel about getting a puppy?"

Harper pauses mid-bite, blinking at me. "A puppy?"

"Yeah." I shrug, leaning back in my chair. "I've been thinking about getting a dog for the farm. And I figured… we could pick one out together."

Her expression is adorable—a mix of surprise and delight, but also… hesitation. "You already have a dog," she points out. "And I can't have pets in my apartment."

"I know," I say easily. "But the puppy would live here at the farm. It'd be yours, but it'd have plenty of space to run around."

She smiles softly, setting down her fork. "That actually sounds really nice."

I grin, but something about the way she says it feels off, like she's thinking about something else entirely… like there's a thought she's not saying out loud. I try not to think about it too much, but there's still some unexpected tension lingering between us when I drop her off at home.

I'm worried I've pushed her too far.

11

UNCOMFORTABLE PASSES

HARPER

Rafe is back in Minnesota to play the Vikings. It's the first game I've gotten to see in person since we all went to San Francisco, and I'm so freaking excited! McKenzy is also buzzing with enthusiasm, bouncing from room to room while we get ready.

"I've already picked out my outfit," she announces from the bathroom, her voice echoing slightly. "It's slutty, but I make it classy."

I laugh, standing in front of my closet, towel still wrapped around me. "I'm sure Rafe's teammates will find you irresistible."

"They'd better," she sings back. "It took a long time to find the perfect balance of the two!"

By the time Damien's sleek black car pulls up to our building, McKenzy and I are both looking fabulous. I went with a body-hugging red dress in the same shade as the 49ers uniforms because Rafe always says red is his favorite color on me. McKenzy, true to form, went for an off-the-shoulder mini-dress in glittering gold that makes her look like a human disco ball.

Damien steps out of the car, looking impeccably tailored, as usual. "Ladies," he greets us, offering each of us an arm. "Ready to make an entrance?"

McKenzy fans herself dramatically. "I might faint. Harper never talks about what a gentleman you are."

Damien smirks. "I'm full of surprises."

When we get to the private box, McKenzy spins around, her arms outstretched, squealing like a kid at Disneyland. This is her first time in the VIP suite, and she's soaking up every inch of it.

"I could get used to this," she says, already pouring herself a mimosa.

I settle into a plush seat right by the glass, my heart leaping the moment I spot Rafe down on the field. He's stretching, talking with his teammates, looking every bit the confident quarterback I fell in love with when we were teenagers.

"See something you like?" Damien murmurs beside me, handing me a glass of champagne.

"I don't know, it's so hard to see from up here," I tease, and Damien kisses me playfully.

Then I turn back to the field, my eyes focused on Rafe.

The game is thrilling. Rafe is in top form, throwing perfect passes, calling plays with the confidence of a seasoned pro. I scream his name every time he does something amazing, and McKenzy joins in even though she barely knows what's happening.

"This is so much better than watching at home," she says between bites of crab cake. "Why didn't you tell me football was fun?"

"Because you always said sports were just sweaty men chasing balls."

"Well, if I knew the sweaty men looked like that–" She gestures toward the field, where Rafe's jersey is clinging to his chest in the most flattering way possible. "I would've paid attention sooner."

The 49ers win, and I swear the whole stadium explodes with noise, even though most of the people here are rooting for the Vikings. I'm on my feet, screaming loud enough to make my throat hurt, and Damien even claps a few times, looking mildly smug. Knowing him, he's probably won a lot of money on the game.

As we leave the stadium, Damien's driver is already waiting, ready to whisk us back to my place so McKenzy and I can change for the after-party.

"Is it weird that I'm more excited for the party than the game?" McKenzy asks, kicking off her heels in the back seat.

"Not even a little bit," I say, still glowing from the excitement of seeing Rafe play so well.

Damien, being Damien, has rented out an entire upscale bar for the party. The place is decked out in red and gold, with 49ers logos everywhere and champagne flowing like water.

McKenzy and I arrive fashionably late, both of us freshly dressed, me in a slinky black number Damien sent over because apparently one dress for the day wasn't sexy enough, and McKenzy in something that looks like it was designed purely to get her noticed.

The second we walk in, I spot Rafe across the room. He's mid-conversation with a couple of teammates, but the moment his eyes land on me, his smile goes soft around the edges, like I'm the only thing he can see.

I melt.

McKenzy, meanwhile, is living her best life. She's already chatting up someone who may or may not be a wide receiver, drink in hand, her laugh loud and uninhibited.

"She's going to end up married to a football player, isn't she?" I say to Rafe, who's got his arm draped casually around my waist.

"I'd rather her chatting him up than you," Rafe admits, kissing the side of my head.

As the night goes on, I notice Damien floating around, doing what he does best, talking to everyone, blending in effortlessly even though he's richer than half the room combined.

He always looks so comfortable, so in control, like this is all just another Sunday night for him.

At one point, I catch him on his phone, voice low, his brows slightly furrowed. I'm close enough to hear snippets of conversation.

"Yeah… covered the spread… told you they'd pull it off…."

My stomach tilts, but not with fear. Because honestly, I'm not surprised. At this point, I'm almost certain Damien is betting on

Rafe's games. And, weirdly, I can't bring myself to care. It's Damien. He lives for risk, for high-stakes moves, for the thrill of control. Besides, it's his money. Who am I to tell him what to do with it?

"Everything okay?" Rafe asks when I drift back to him after watching Damien.

"Yeah," I say, leaning into his side. "Just... taking it all in."

He kisses the top of my head, his fingers tracing lazy circles on my hip. "I'm glad you're here."

"Me too."

The party hums around me, a blur of laughter, clinking glasses, and the bass thumping through the floorboards like a second heartbeat.

Rafe goes off to talk with a group of guys near the bar, his smile wide and easy, the kind of smile I don't think I saw once during the months we were apart. McKenzy is somewhere, probably dancing with the kicker she's been flirting with all night.

Which leaves me, for the first time tonight, alone.

I weave through the crowd, looking for a familiar face, my drink clenched tightly in one hand. The dress Damien picked out for me hugs me in all the right places, but now I feel exposed instead of glamorous, like every pair of eyes I pass lingers a little too long.

I make it halfway to the bar before someone steps in front of me.

"Hey there," a deep voice calls to me over the music.

I look up and find myself face-to-face with Jeff McNaught, Rafe's second-string quarterback–the same guy who eyed me weirdly when Rafe introduced me to his teammates. He's drunk, his smile too wide, his eyes glassy.

"Uh, hey," I say, taking a step back, but the crowd behind me doesn't budge, leaving me trapped between him and a wall of bodies.

"You look–" He lets his gaze drip down my body like spilled whiskey. "Fucking incredible tonight."

"Thanks," I say, trying to slide past him, but he blocks my path.

"You and Maloney," he says, his grin turning sour. "That's still a thing, huh?"

"Very much a thing." I smile tightly, hoping he gets the hint.

But he doesn't. Instead, he leans closer, the reek of alcohol rolling off him in waves.

"You know, I always wondered what it'd be like to get a taste of the girl who brought Rafe to his knees."

My stomach turns. "Excuse me?" I try to sound confident, but my voice comes out too soft, too uncertain.

Jeff's smile widens, reaching for my waist, and I freeze for half a second, unsure whether to slap him or scream.

"Step away from her." Rafe's voice is sharp, cutting through the noise like a blade.

Jeff drops his hand immediately, his face going pale as Rafe steps between us, his shoulders tense, jaw clenched tight enough to shatter.

"She's with me," Rafe says, his tone leaving no room for argument.

Jeff holds up both hands in mock surrender. "Hey, man, we were just talking."

"Talk to someone else." Rafe doesn't move, his stance protective, his hand curling around my wrist to pull me gently behind him.

Jeff opens his mouth like he's going to say something, probably something stupid, but then he thinks better of it and turns, vanishing back into the crowd. The second he's gone, I let out a tense breath.

"You okay?" Rafe asks, turning toward me, his hand sliding to my lower back.

"I'm fine," I say, even though my heart is still pounding.

"He didn't–"

"No." I cut him off quickly. "He was just drunk and gross."

Rafe's jaw flexes, his hand tightening slightly against me, and for a moment, I think he's going to go after Jeff. But then he looks at me, and whatever anger was building softens into something else.

"Let's get you a drink." He leads me toward the bar, his touch alone erasing what just happened.

The rest of the party blurs into dancing, laughing, and champagne that bubbles in my veins.

Rafe keeps me close after that, his hand never straying far from my waist, his gaze constantly flickering toward me like he's afraid I'll disappear if he looks away too long. I love him for that. But I also know he's still processing what happened.

I make a mental note to talk to him about it later when we're alone.

It's late at night when the party finally starts to wind down. Many of the players left earlier to catch the team flight back to California, though some stayed behind and will leave in the morning. Rafe's off with his teammates, I don't know where McKenzy is, and I find myself wandering onto the balcony, drawn to the quiet like a moth to flame. That's where I find Damien.

He's leaning against the railing, his jacket slung over his shoulder, his tie undone, hair slightly mussed like someone's been running fingers through it.

"You hiding out here?" I ask, stepping beside him.

He turns, his smile slow and lazy. "I could ask you the same."

I shrug, the cool night air sending a shiver down my spine.

"Cold?"

"A little."

He drapes his jacket around my shoulders without a word, his fingers lingering at the collar, brushing my skin just enough to make me shiver again for a very different reason.

"You know," I say softly, turning to face him. "You've been unusually well-behaved tonight."

He smirks. "Maybe I'm turning over a new leaf."

"Doubtful."

He chuckles, and before I can overthink it, I rise onto my toes and kiss him.

It starts soft, sweet even, but then Damien's hands slide into my hair, pulling me closer, and the kiss deepens, heat flaring between us like a spark catching dry wood.

For a second, I forget where we are, who could see us, and just let myself fall into him. When we finally pull apart, my lips feel swollen, my heart racing.

"Consider that your goodnight kiss," I whisper.

"Remind me to behave more often," Damien says, voice low.

Damien tells me goodbye and heads out to where his driver is waiting for him, and by the time Rafe, McKenzy, and I pile into an Uber, I'm exhausted.

McKenzy leans her head on my shoulder, half-asleep already, and Rafe's arm is draped across the back of the seat, his fingers idly tracing the nape of my neck.

The car hums softly, the city lights blurring past the windows, and for the first time in days, I feel something like peace settle over me.

"You okay?" Rafe asks, voice soft.

"Yeah," I say. "Just tired."

He squeezes my thigh. "Me, too."

When we pull up to the apartment, McKenzy stumbles sleepily inside with a lazy wave. Rafe and I disappear to my room, and the second the door closes behind us, I exhale. It's quiet, just the two of us, and I bask in the intimacy. Rafe pulls me into his arms, holding me close, his chin resting on top of my head.

"I missed this," I murmur.

"Me too."

We strip off our clothes down to our underwear and fall into bed, limbs tangled, the scent of champagne, sweat, and leftover adrenaline still clinging to our skin. I fall asleep with his heart beating under my ear, his hand curled protectively around my waist.

1 2

A GOOD GIRL

A few days later, Rafe calls mid-morning, his voice soft and a little guilty, like he's been sitting with something too heavy for too long.

"Hey," he says when I answer. "You got a minute?"

I sink into the couch, tucking my legs under me and feeling oddly nervous.

"Of course."

There's a short pause, but long enough for me to know this isn't just a casual check-in.

"I've been thinking about the party," he says. "About McNaught."

I close my eyes briefly. "Rafe—"

"No, just let me say this." His voice is firm, but there's worry underneath. "I should've shut that down before it even started. I knew he was weird about me taking the starting spot, and I saw how he was looking at you when I introduced you. I just didn't think–"

"That he'd corner me?" I finish for him.

"Yeah." His sigh is heavy. "That's on me."

"No," I say, keeping my voice gentle. "That's on him. You're not responsible for what some jealous creep does after too many drinks."

He goes quiet for a second. "I still feel like I should've protected you better."

My heart squeezes. "You did protect me, Rafe. You showed up exactly when I needed you. That's what matters."

There's another silence, but this one feels lighter. "I miss you already," he says.

"Same," I tell him honestly, a lump forming in my throat.

We talk a little longer, nothing heavy, just the comfortable stuff. He tells me how practice is going, what he had for breakfast, how his nutritionist has him on a new regimen. I tell him how McKenzy has started repurposing old tables into plant holders all over the apartment. By the time we hang up, my chest feels a little less tight, like I've let go of a knot in my chest that had been there undetected since the party.

A knock on the door comes just as I'm reheating my coffee for the third time. McKenzy looks up from her latest furniture rehab project, a battered nightstand she's trying to turn into a bar cart.

"Are we expecting someone?"

"I'm not." I wipe my hands on a dish towel and answer the door.

A delivery guy is standing there, holding a sleek black box tied with a lavender ribbon.

"Delivery for Harper Ward," he says, and I barely manage a "thanks" before he's already halfway down the hall.

McKenzy leans over my shoulder as I set the small box on the counter. "Ooh, mysterious."

I pull the ribbon, the lid popping open with a soft whoosh. Inside, nestled in velvet, is a single silver key.

Under the key is a note, written in elegant calligraphy:

"Take McKenzy. Go to this address. - Damien"

McKenzy grabs the card, squinting at the address. "He is so extra."

I grin, my heart fluttering in that way it always does when Damien decides to drop surprises out of nowhere. "Let's go."

The address leads to a building I've never seen before, tucked between a pottery studio and a boutique that sells handmade soap shaped like corgis. It's beautiful, all exposed brick and huge windows, the kind of place that looks like it was meant for artists.

McKenzy bounces on her toes, her energy palpable. "Please tell me this is what I think it is."

I slide the key into the lock and turn. The door opens smoothly, and we step inside.

"Oh my God." We both squeal at the same time.

It's perfect. The space is open and bright, with wide wooden floors, high ceilings, and enough natural light to make a painter cry. One side has shelves and tables perfect for McKenzy's furniture projects. The other side is a dream studio, easels already set up, blank canvases waiting like they've been calling my name.

There's a kitchen, too, fully stocked because, of course, Damien thought of that. Snacks line the counters, the fridge is full of every drink we love, and there's even a liquor cabinet because, apparently, creativity needs fuel.

"This can't be real," McKenzy whispers.

But it is… because Damien made it real. We wander the space, laughing, pointing out every detail like we've won the artistic lottery.

"Look at this light!" McKenzy practically hugs the window. "My pieces are going to look so good in here."

I spin in the center of the room, my arms wide. "We have a studio."

"Our own studio," she adds, shaking her head like she still can't believe it.

I feel my phone buzz, and when I check, it's Damien calling. "Perfect timing," I say, answering. "How the hell did you find this place?"

He chuckles, low and rich. "A magician never reveals his secrets."

"Well, thank you," I say, meaning every word. "This is incredible."

"I'm glad you like it." His voice softens just slightly. "Are you free tonight? I'd like to take you to dinner."

I glance at McKenzy, who's already giving me a thumbs up. "Absolutely."

"Good. My driver will pick you up at seven."

Damien

Harper steps out of the elevator into the dimly lit hallway, and I have to remind myself to breathe.

"Holy Fuck," I murmur, closing the distance between us in two strides.

Her smile is all trouble. "That good, huh?"

"Little red bird, if you don't want me to bend you over this hallway table and ruin you before we even make it to dinner, you should probably stop smiling like that."

Her eyes flick down to my mouth, and her tongue peeks out just enough to make me want to bite it. "Noted."

I slide her coat off her shoulders, letting my fingers brush her skin as I help her into the limo. The driver already knows where we're going. It's the most exclusive restaurant in town, where the staff practically worship me. I could have had dinner catered in my penthouse, but tonight, I want to show her off—let every man in that room see exactly who she belongs to.

Inside the limo, Harper's leg brushes against mine. I glance down and see the way her dress has ridden up, exposing the smooth curve of her thighs. I trail my fingers along her skin, watching as goosebumps bloom beneath my touch.

"You wore this for me," I say, my voice low.

She grins. "Obviously."

"Such a good girl."

Her breath catches, and just like that, the air between us shifts from playful to charged.

I lean in, brushing my lips along her ear. "I hope you remember who you belong to tonight."

Her voice is barely a whisper. "I never forget."

The restaurant goes silent the moment we step inside, not out of rudeness, but because when a man like me walks in with a woman like her, people notice. Harper holds my arm, her fingers resting lightly on my sleeve, and I feel the subtle tremor in her touch. It's not fear. It's excitement. She loves being on display just as much as I love showing her off.

I guide her to our private table in the back, away from prying eyes but still visible enough for the right kind of attention. The sommelier appears immediately, offering a bottle I imported specifically for tonight.

Harper lifts her glass, and we toast.

"To the most beautiful woman in the room," I say.

She blushes. "You're biased."

"Damn right I am."

She takes a sip, her tongue flicking out to catch a stray drop of wine from her lower lip. I grip the edge of the table, fighting the urge to drag her into my lap right there.

"You know," I murmur, my fingers tracing circles on the back of her hand, "if you keep looking at me like that, I'm going to have to do something about it."

"Like what?" Her eyes flash with that dangerous curiosity I love so much.

I lean in, my lips brushing her ear. "Like make you come right here at this table."

Her breath catches, her thighs pressing together under the tablecloth. "You wouldn't."

I slide my hand beneath the table, resting it lightly on her knee. "Wouldn't I?"

She swallows hard, but she doesn't stop me.

"Spread your legs, little red bird." My voice is so soft no one else can hear, but she feels the command like a touch.

Her gaze darts around the room, checking to make sure no one's looking. They're not. Our table is perfectly angled, just private enough for my hand to disappear under the slit of her dress without anyone noticing.

"Now," I say, squeezing her thigh.

She obeys, slowly parting her legs beneath the table. I drag my fingers up her inner thigh, tracing soft patterns on her skin, until I find what I'm looking for.

"Fuck," I whisper, my cock instantly hard. "No panties?"

She grins, biting her lip. I slide my fingers between her folds, finding her already slick and warm for me. I move my fingers slowly, teasing, barely there. Harper's breath stutters, her back arching ever so slightly, and I know I've got her exactly where I want her.

"Be still," I order softly, rubbing slow, lazy circles over her clit. "Smile. Looks like nothing's happening."

Her smile is a little too bright, her eyes a little too wide, and I know she's fighting to keep it together.

"You're evil," she whispers.

"You love it."

She's right. I *am* evil. Because I keep touching her, slow and deliberate, until her thighs tremble beneath my hand. I slip a finger inside her, then two, curling them just right until I feel her tighten around me.

"Damien," she breathes, gripping the edge of the tablecloth so tight her knuckles go white.

"Shh." I press my thumb to her clit, flicking gently. "Be a good girl and come for me."

Her orgasm hits so fast she bites her lip to keep from crying out. I feel every flutter, every pulse, every desperate clench around my fingers, and it's the most beautiful fucking thing.

When she finally opens her eyes again, they're glassy and dazed. I lift my fingers to my mouth, licking them clean with a wicked grin.

"Best appetizer I've ever had," I say.

Her blush could light the whole damn room.

"Now," I smirk, signaling the waiter, "let's order dinner."

Later, when we step into the penthouse, I have her pressed against the door, my mouth crashing down on hers. She tastes like wine and strawberries, and I'm starving for her.

Her hands go to my shirt, fumbling with buttons, but I grab her wrists and pin them above her head.

"Not tonight," I say, voice rough. "Tonight, you're mine to unwrap."

She whimpers, exactly the sound I wanted, and my cock aches painfully against my zipper.

"Say it," I demand.

"I'm yours, baby."

"Good girl."

Her breath catches as I press her against the glass wall of my penthouse, her back arching into me, her hips already rolling forward like her body knows exactly what I want from her. She's so damn responsive, my perfect little red bird. Always eager to please me. I slip the straps of her dress off her shoulders, letting the silk slide down her body like water over skin, pooling at her feet. No bra. No panties. Just like I like her.

"You wore this for me," I murmur, my fingers trailing down her spine.

She shivers. "Yes, Damien."

"Good girl."

I spin her around, my hands framing her face as I kiss her deep and slow, possessive. She melts into me, her body soft and pliant, trusting me to take her exactly how I need to.

"Hands on the glass," I command, voice low.

She obeys without hesitation, pressing her palms flat against the window. The city sprawls out below us, glittering and oblivious to the sin happening high above.

I step back just enough to admire her—naked, glowing in the city light, her body mine to do with as I please.

"Look at you," I murmur, trailing my fingers down her back. "So pretty, all laid out for me."

She shifts her weight, just slightly, thighs pressing together in search of friction.

"Stay still," I order.

She freezes, her breath hitching. I love that she needs me like this, that I've ruined her for soft and sweet, made her crave the sharp edge of being told exactly what to do. My hand drifts lower, fingers skimming between her legs, finding her already soaked for me.

"Such a messy little thing," I tease. "Were you wet all through dinner, too?"

She nods, forehead resting against the glass. "I always am when I'm with you."

"Of course you are."

I slip two fingers inside her without warning, feeling her body clench down immediately, and fuck, she's so tight and warm, so perfectly mine. She gasps, her back arching, but she keeps her hands on the glass just like I told her.

"Good girl," I praise, bending my fingers, dragging them slowly over that sweet spot inside her until her knees start to shake.

"Please, baby," she whispers.

"Please what?"

"Please fuck me."

I withdraw my fingers, slick and glistening, and press them to her lips.

"Clean them off first." Her tongue flicks out, obedient and filthy, and my cock throbs at the sight. I step back just long enough to unbutton my shirt, tossing it aside before stripping off my pants. My cock springs free, already leaking at the tip, desperate for the heat of her body.

"Damien," she whimpers, shifting her weight again.

"What did I say about staying still?" I growl.

She freezes. "Sorry, baby."

I press my chest against her back, my cock sliding between her thighs, slicking up with her wetness. "Don't move unless I tell you to."

"Yes, baby."

I drag my teeth along her neck, nipping just hard enough to make her yelp. Then, in one smooth thrust, I bury myself inside her, stretching her wide, filling her completely. She cries out, her fingers clawing at the glass, but she doesn't break the rules. She stays right where I put her, taking every inch like the good girl she is.

"God, you're perfect," I groan, pulling back and slamming into her again, setting a hard, relentless rhythm that shakes the window.

Her reflection stares back at me, cheeks flushed, lips parted, eyes glazed with lust and submission.

"Look at you," I murmur in her ear. "My perfect little red bird, taking my cock so well."

"Please—" she gasps, her body trembling. "Please touch me." I slide one hand between her legs, my fingers circling her clit in tight little circles, and her body shudders immediately.

"Don't come until I say," I warn.

She bites her lip, desperate to obey. Her body clamps down around me, her walls fluttering, so close I can feel it, and fuck, I love holding her there, right on the edge, waiting for me to decide if she's earned it.

"You've been a good girl tonight," I mutter, nipping at her shoulder. "Go ahead. Come for me."

She breaks apart, crying out my name as her body milks me, her orgasm rolling through her like a storm. I don't stop. I keep thrusting, chasing my own release, until I feel that familiar tightness coiling in my spine.

"Where do you want me, little red bird?"

"Inside," she gasps. "Please, baby, fill me up."

I thrust deep, grinding against her, and let go, spilling into her with a low, filthy groan. We stand there, pressed against the glass, panting and wrecked, the city glittering beneath us like a silent witness to our sin.

"Do you see how beautiful you are when you come?" I murmur, my hand sliding up to cup her breast, fingers tweaking her nipple just enough to make her whimper.

"Yes, baby," she whispers.

"Good girl."

13

SHOWDOWN ON THE PORCH

I don't plan to take Harper to the salsa club tonight. It's our place, our little pocket of rhythm and heat where we move together like our bodies were made to match. But it's also somewhere Carmen knows I'll be. And lately, I can't shake the feeling that she isn't done making trouble for us. So I call Harper and suggest something different.

"A jazz club?" she repeats, sounding both surprised and intrigued.

"Sí," I say, smiling into the phone. "It's not as spicy, but it has its own kind of heat. You'll see."

She laughs, soft and sweet, and I already know tonight is going to be perfect.

When I pull up to her apartment, she's already waiting outside, wearing a silky black dress that clings to her curves like it was painted on. Her hair tumbles over her shoulders in soft waves, her lips painted a deep red that's already staining my imagination.

"Dios mío," I murmur, stepping out to open the passenger door for her. "You are dangerous, mi preciosa."

She smiles, slow and knowing, and slides into the seat like a queen settling onto her throne. "You say that every time."

"Because it's always true."

The drive to the club is easy, full of teasing and laughter, her hand resting on my thigh like it belongs there. I want to pull over and kiss her senseless, but I also want to show her off, walk into the club with her on my arm and let everyone know that the most beautiful woman in the room is with me.

The club is dark, moody, filled with low music and the kind of atmosphere that invites secrets to be whispered against collarbones. We slip into a small table near the stage, and Harper leans in close, her bare knee brushing against mine.

"This is nice," she says, her voice softer than usual. "Different."

"I wanted to try something new." I glance toward the door, but no one unexpectedly walks in. "Somewhere we can just enjoy each other."

She studies me for a second, her smile dimming just slightly. "You're worried about her, aren't you?"

There's no need to ask who. "A little," I admit. "I just want tonight to be about us."

Harper squeezes my hand. "Then it will be."

And for the next two hours, it is.

We drink good wine and listen to jazz that melts into our bones. Harper sways in her seat, her eyes half-closed, and I can't take my eyes off her. The candlelight flickers over her skin, her dress riding higher every time she crosses her legs.

By the time the last set ends, I'm aching to have her.

"Come home with me," I whisper against her ear, letting my lips graze her skin.

She shivers, and it's the sexiest thing I've ever seen.

The drive to my house is full of anticipation, her hand sliding higher on my thigh, my fingers tracing the inside of her wrist. I can barely focus on the road, and by the time we pull into my driveway, I'm half ready to take her in the car.

But then I see the figure on my porch.

Carmen.

"Shit," I mutter, my hand tightening on the steering wheel.

Harper follows my gaze, her expression wary. "Is that...?"

"Sí," I say tightly. "Stay here."

Of course, she doesn't.

The moment I step out, Harper's door opens, too, and she's right behind me, her bare shoulders straight, chin lifted... my brave, beautiful girl.

"Ah, the little whore is here, too," Carmen slurs, a wine bottle dangling from her fingers. "How perfect."

Harper

I'VE HAD MY FAIR SHARE OF AWKWARD ENCOUNTERS IN MY LIFE, BUT standing half-shielded behind Tomas, in heels and a dress meant for jazz and cocktails, while his drunk ex-wife screams obscenities at me?

This one takes the cake.

Carmen's makeup is smudged, her dress askew, her hair unraveling from the tight bun she probably spent an hour perfecting. She looks nothing like the polished professor I remember or even the jealous ex-wife I've encountered before

Her eyes are full of fire and venom, locked on me like I'm the reason the sun set on her entire life. Never mind that she's the one who ended things with Tomas.

His hand stays firm on my waist, holding me close, but I can feel the tension rolling off him. He's trying to stay calm, but his jaw is clenched so tight I'm honestly surprised he hasn't shattered a tooth.

"You're a cheap whore," Carmen slurs, pointing a trembling finger at me. "Ruining a good man's life for your own little ego trip."

I pull out my phone, thumb shaking only slightly, and start

recording because if she's going to treat me like this, I want proof. Tomas glances at me, briefly surprised, but I see the flicker of approval when he realizes what I'm doing.

"Carmen," Tomas says, voice low and controlled, but there's a dangerous edge to it, "go home. Right now."

Carmen laughs, but it's the kind of sound that doesn't belong on a front porch on what was a nice evening. It belongs in a psych ward. "Why? So you can keep screwing this little artsy slut? I wonder how the university would feel if I told them you were fucking one of your former students." Her voice cracks at the end, and for half a second, I almost feel bad for her. Almost. Because then she lunges, actually lunges, at me, swiping at my face with her claws. Tomas blocks her with one smooth motion, his arm snapping out like a wall between us.

"Enough." His voice is thunder, echoing down the quiet street.

Carmen staggers back, suddenly realizing the scene she's making.

"This is attempted assault," Tomas says, pulling out his phone. "I'm calling the police."

"No!" Carmen shrieks. "Tomas, please—"

But he's already dialing, his hand still firm against my back. "Yes, I need to report an incident. Harassment, attempted assault. Yes, we're outside my home."

Carmen stumbles back another step, her desperation turning sour. "You can't do this to me!"

"You did this to yourself," Tomas replies coldly.

The police arrive quickly, and I'm honestly grateful for the speed. The whole time, I keep filming, holding my phone steady even when my heart feels like it's trying to climb out of my throat.

The police are polite but firm, separating Carmen from us and asking Tomas to explain what happened. I hand over my recording, showing the whole messy incident from the first slur to the almost-slap. Carmen tries to play the victim at first, crying and telling the officers I'm a home wrecker who seduced her husband. But when the video contradicts every word, her sobs turn to screaming again, and she actually tries to kick one of the officers. That's the moment they decide she's spending the night in the drunk tank.

"Ms. Ward," one of the officers says, turning toward me as Carmen is handcuffed and led toward the squad car, "I'd strongly recommend you file a restraining order. This isn't likely to end tonight."

I nod, my hands still shaking a little as I tuck my phone into my clutch. "Yeah. Yeah, I will. Thank you."

Once they're gone, Tomas stands on the porch, hands on his hips, staring out at the empty street.

"You okay?" I ask softly, stepping beside him.

He lets out a long, slow breath, running a hand through his hair. "I knew she was unhinged, but this…."

"She needs help," I say, even though I'm still mad as hell.

"She does." His arm slides around my waist, pulling me into his side. "But that doesn't mean she gets to hurt you."

I lean into him, my cheek resting against his shoulder. "I'm okay," I whisper, even though my heart is still racing, and my skin feels too tight, like it's holding in more than my body can contain.

Tomas kisses the top of my head, his lips lingering there longer than necessary, like he's silently apologizing for Carmen's insanity, for ever letting her into his life in the first place. "Let's go inside," he says softly, his hand never leaving mine.

The second the door closes, Tomas's hands are on me. Grabbing. Pulling. Claiming. Like he's trying to erase every filthy word Carmen spat at me and replace them with nothing but his touch.

I melt into him immediately because this is where I feel safest, under his hands, under his body, surrounded by his warmth, strength, and devotion.

"Let me take care of you," he whispers, his voice rough and desperate.

"You already do," I whisper back, and it's the truth. He always has.

We don't even make it to the bedroom. We barely make it past the door before he's pushing me back onto the couch, his hands sliding up my thighs, fingers curling under the hem of my dress and shoving it up to my waist.

"You're mine," he says between kisses, his lips trailing fire down my neck, over my collarbone, until he's sucking a mark onto my skin that'll still be there tomorrow.

"I'm yours," I agree, breathless and needy, my fingers already working the buttons of his shirt.

There's nothing slow or careful about this. It's not the gentle lovemaking we've shared in candlelit bedrooms. This is urgent, driven by fear and fury and the bone-deep relief that we're still standing together after everything.

Tomas is all heat, muscle, and hands that hold me like I'm precious even when he's rough. His shirt hits the floor, and I run my hands over his chest, tracing the lines of muscle, feeling the power under his skin.

He grabs my wrists, pinning them above my head with one hand while the other slides my panties down my legs. He doesn't even bother taking my dress off, just pushes it higher, until the fabric is bunched around my ribs, leaving me exposed and trembling beneath him.

"You're so fucking beautiful," he murmurs, his mouth descending on my breast, tongue flicking my nipple, sucking hard until I arch into him. "Carmen could never touch this."

I whimper, my hips bucking against him, desperate for friction. "Please, Profe."

He groans at the nickname, his cock pressing hard against his pants.

"Helena," he rasps, "you make me so fucking loco."

I reach between us, popping the button on his pants, shoving them down with greedy hands until his cock springs free, thick, heavy, already leaking at the tip. My mouth waters, but I need him inside me more than I need to taste him right now.

Tomas runs the head of his dick through my folds, coating himself in my slickness, teasing my clit until I'm writhing beneath him.

"You're always so wet for me," he murmurs. "Always ready."

"Because I know what's coming," I pant, legs spreading wider to welcome him. "And I want all of it."

He lines up at my entrance, and I brace myself, because Tomas is girthy. His cock makes me feel split open in the best possible way, leaves me sore and satisfied for days. He pushes inside, slowly at first, and I gasp, my fingers digging into his shoulders. No matter how many times we do this, I'll never get used to how he stretches me. It's too much and exactly enough all at once.

"Helena," he groans, forehead pressed to mine, "you're so tight. Always so fucking tight."

"More," I whisper, my legs wrapping around his waist, heels digging into his back to pull him deeper. "I need all of you."

He thrusts all the way in, his hips flush against mine, and we both moan at the exquisite stretch. My body struggles to accommodate him, but I crave the slight sting, the way he makes me feel completely *claimed.*

"Good girl," he praises, brushing a kiss to my temple. "Taking me so well."

His hands grip my hips, hard enough to leave fingerprints, and he starts to move. Each thrust is deliberate, deep, his thick length dragging along every nerve ending inside me. I cling to him, my nails raking down his back, leaving my own marks in return.

"You feel so fucking good," he rasps. "So perfect."

He shifts his angle, tilting my hips higher, and the new position makes his cock rub against that sweet spot that has me seeing stars. My breath catches, my back arching as pleasure builds faster than I can control.

"Tomas," I gasp, my body already tightening around him.

"I've got you," he whispers, his forehead pressed to mine, sweat beading along his brow. "I've always got you."

His hand slides between us, fingers finding my clit, rubbing in slow, dirty circles until I shatter beneath him, my orgasm slamming into me like a wave. I cry out his name, and the sound of it, raw and desperate, pulls him over the edge with me.

"Helena," he groans, his hips snapping forward one last time before he spills inside me, his cock pulsing deep, filling me with his heat.

He collapses against me, his weight comforting instead of crushing, his face buried in my neck. I stroke his hair, my fingers tracing lazy circles on his scalp as our breathing slowly syncs back up.

"I meant it, you know," he says softly. "You're mine. Nothing Carmen says or does can change that."

"I know." I kiss his temple. "And you're mine, Profe."

He lifts his head just enough to kiss me, slow this time, tender, filled with all the things neither of us is quite ready to say out loud..

After, we lay tangled together, his fingers tracing circles on my back, both of us too wired to sleep but too tired to move.

"You still wanna file that restraining order?" he asks softly.

"Definitely."

The next morning, we're at the police station before they even finish their first pot of coffee.

The officer from the night before is there, greeting us with a nod. "Good to see you again," he says, though his tone makes it clear he wishes it were under different circumstances.

Filing the paperwork is weirdly surreal. I never imagined myself needing a restraining order against a lover's ex-wife. But here we are.

Tomas holds my hand the entire time, his thumb sweeping over my knuckles every time I start to tense up.

When it's all over, the officer hands me a copy with a sympathetic smile. "We'll submit this to the judge. After an arrest like this, he usually signs off quickly, and you'll get a copy of the final order in the mail. Hopefully, this is the last time you need to deal with her."

"Hopefully," I agree.

But something in my gut tells me Carmen isn't done yet. As we step back into the morning sunlight, Tomas pulls me to a stop, his hands framing my face. "Thank you."

"For what?"

"For not running," he says softly. "For standing by me even though my past got ugly."

I smile, leaning up to kiss him. "We all have messy pasts, Tomas. It's what we do next that matters."

His smile is slow, but genuine. "What do you want to do next, Helena?"

I wrap my arms around his neck, standing on my toes to whisper into his ear. "You owe me a round two."

He laughs, sweeping me into his arms.

14

MILO

Harper

My phone rings as I'm balancing a coffee mug in one hand and my sketchpad in the other. I almost ignore it, but the Chicago area code catches my eye. It's the Whitney Gallery. I set everything down and grab my phone just before the call rolls to voicemail. "Hello?"

"Hi, is this Harper Ward?"

"This is she."

"This is Stephanie from the Whitney Gallery in Chicago. I'm calling with some incredible news."

I blink, my heart leaping into my throat. "Go on," I squeak out, annoyed by how amateur I sound.

"We sold your piece," she says, her voice bubbling with excitement. "It went for considerably more than the asking price. You'll be receiving a huge check from us."

"Oh, my God," I breathe, my knees weakening until I have to lean against the counter. "That's… wow. That's amazing."

"It's well deserved," Stephanie says warmly. "We'd love to have more of your work if you're interested."

"I'm definitely interested," I manage, my mind spinning.

We wrap up the call, and when I hang up, I just stand there for a moment, absorbing it all. I did it. I really, truly did it.

McKenzy bursts into the kitchen, mid-rant about the hardware store guy who hit on her when she went to pick up new knobs for a dresser. She stops when she sees my face. "Uh-oh. What's that look?"

I grin so wide it hurts. "They sold my painting."

McKenzy screams, grabbing my hands and jumping up and down like a lunatic. "Harper! That's amazing! How much?"

I tell her what I know, and she freezes. "Shut. Up."

"Not shutting up."

"That's… oh, my God." She spins around in a circle, then points at me. "You know what this calls for?"

"Celebratory snacks?"

"No. Studio time."

We practically race to the studio, McKenzy hauling her tools and paints, me juggling canvases and a box of new brushes.

The place already feels like home, even though we've only been working here a few weeks. The sunlight spills across the floors, the smell of paint and sawdust mingling in the air, and it feels like I'm exactly where I'm supposed to be.

McKenzy cranks up our favorite playlist, and we both dive into our work, the energy buzzing between us.

I throw paint onto a fresh canvas, no plan, just pure release. Every emotion, from the pride in selling my painting to my worries about Carmen, to my annoyance at Rafe's teammate, to my curiosity about Damien's secret calls, and finally my anxiety about Scott's feelings, pours out in color and shape.

McKenzy hums along to the music, sanding down the top of a vintage vanity she's restoring, her face smudged with sawdust but glowing with happiness. For a while, there's only the sound of brushes scraping canvas, sandpaper smoothing wood, and the occasional burst of laughter when one of us accidentally makes a mess.

Later, during a break, we sit in the tiny kitchenette, eating peanut butter out of the jar and drinking canned cocktails from Damien's impossibly well-stocked fridge.

McKenzy gestures at my half-finished painting, her brow furrowed. "This one feels different."

"Different how?"

She shrugs. "It's bolder. More chaotic. Like you had a lot on your mind."

I twirl my spoon in the peanut butter, my stomach twisting. "I do."

McKenzy narrows her eyes. "Is this about Scott again?"

"Maybe."

She sighs dramatically, flopping back against the stool. "Harper, I love you, but you are the queen of overthinking. So the man wants to adopt a puppy with you. It sounds like he's doing all the work taking care of it. What's the big deal?"

"I just–" I pause, chewing my lip. "I'm worried he's starting to want more. Like, sure, today it's a puppy. But what if tomorrow he wants to talk about having babies?"

McKenzy rolls her eyes. "Did he say that?"

"No."

"Has he hinted at that at all?"

"Not really."

McKenzy spreads her arms wide. "Then what the hell are you even stressing about?"

I stir my drink with a different spoon. "It's just the vibe sometimes. He invites me to family stuff. Talks about puppies. Looks at me like–"

"Like you hung the moon?" McKenzy finishes.

"Yeah."

She leans forward, poking my forehead with her finger. "Harper. Not every man who cares about you secretly wants to slap a ring on your finger and lock you in a house with a picket fence."

"I know that."

"Do you?"

I sigh. "I'm just scared."

"Of what?"

"Losing him."

McKenzy softens, setting her spoon down. "Honey, you're not

going to lose Scott. He knew what he was signing up for when this all started. If he ever wants to talk about changing things, he'll talk to you. Until then, maybe try enjoying what you have instead of inventing problems."

I laugh despite myself. "You make it sound so easy."

"Because it is."

We head back to our respective projects, but McKenzy's words linger. She's right. Scott has never once pressured me for anything I didn't want to give. He's been supportive, open, patient, and as far as boyfriends go, he's pretty damn perfect.

So why am I so scared?

I lose track of time in the paint, my brush moving faster than my thoughts, color bleeding into color until the canvas is a riot of feeling. The studio door creaks open, and I glance over my shoulder to see Scott standing there, looking slightly sheepish.

"Hey," he says with an excited gleam in his eye. "Are you ready to go pick out our new baby?"

McKenzy bursts out laughing hysterically, and I can't help but blush. "I can't wait to meet your new child," she calls as we walk out together.

Scott

I KNEW THE SECOND I SUGGESTED GETTING A PUPPY TOGETHER THAT I'D probably gone too far. But I couldn't help it. The idea popped into my head while Harper was asleep beside me, her hair spilling across my pillow, her hand resting on my chest like it belonged there, and all I could think about was how easy it is with her, how much I want her to be part of everything, even the quiet, everyday stuff like lazy Sundays, puppy kisses, and mornings spent sitting on the porch with coffee while a dog chases butterflies across the grass. Maybe it's cheesy, but with Harper, even the cheesy stuff feels right.

"So, where are we going first?" she asks as we leave her studio.

"I made a list," I say, handing her my phone. "Different breeds, different places. We'll visit a few and see who we click with."

Her eyes soften as she scrolls. "You put a lot of thought into this."

"Of course, I did." I pull onto the highway, heading toward the first kennel. "It's not every day you get a co-parenting opportunity with the girl of your dreams."

Harper tenses a bit, but her smile doesn't falter. I catch the slight change, though. Ever since she left last time, I've been overthinking every single interaction. I can only hope getting the puppy will help. Maybe she's just worried about the responsibility, but once we take him or her home, she'll see that I'm committed to doing the majority of the work.

The first kennel is pure chaos—puppies everywhere, rolling, yipping, tumbling over each other in a furry explosion of joy. Harper kneels down immediately, letting a whole gang of them swarm her, her laughter ringing out so loud and clear it makes my heart ache.

"Do you want a boy or a girl?" I ask, crouching beside her.

She lifts a tiny golden retriever puppy onto her lap, the pup immediately licking her chin.

"I don't care," she says. "I just want to give it a million kisses."

We visit three more places after that, meeting a parade of perfect puppies, but it's the fourth stop at a small, family-run rescue where we find the one.

He's a little black and white mutt, all floppy ears and wiggly tail, with one blue eye and one brown eye. The second Harper picks him up, he curls into her neck, sighing like he's just found his person.

"This is the one," she whispers, her voice a little choked up.

I stroke the pup's head, my chest tight in the best way. "Yeah. He's perfect."

The drive back to my place is full of puppy talk, names, training plans, questions over where he'll sleep… my bed, obviously.

"He needs a name," Harper says, cradling him in her lap as he snoozes.

"You pick," I say. "He's yours as much as mine."

She thinks for a minute, then grins. "Milo."

"Milo," I repeat, glancing at the rearview mirror where his tiny reflection is visible. "Perfect."

At home, Milo explores every corner, his tail wagging so hard his whole butt wiggles with it. Harper follows him around, snapping pictures and giggling every time he trips over his own feet.

Watching them together, my girl and my dog, something in my chest clicks into place. This feels like home. With Milo here, she seems back to her old self, so I finally feel my anxiety ease a little. When Milo finally tuckers himself out and collapses in the bed we've set up for him by the fireplace, I lead her back to my bedroom.

Harper takes her clothes off and lies back on my bed, her skin glowing in the firelight spilling in from the other room. sprawled out like an invitation, her legs just slightly parted, waiting for me.

And hell if that doesn't make me feel like the luckiest man alive.

I crawl over her, my hands bracing beside her head, but she catches me by the belt loops before I can fully settle.

"Lose these," she says, tugging gently at my jeans.

"Yes, ma'am."

I stand just long enough to strip, her eyes drinking me in, her teeth tugging at her lower lip like she's already imagining all the ways I'm about to wreck her. When I climb back onto the bed naked, she pulls me down, her hands sliding over my chest, tracing the ridges of muscle and the lines worn into my skin from a lifetime of farm work.

"I missed this," she whispers, her fingers dancing down to my hips, then lower, wrapping around my cock with that perfect grip that's somehow soft and firm at the same time.

"Careful," I groan, my forehead resting against hers. "You get me too worked up, and this is gonna end before it starts."

She grins, but I capture her mouth before she can get a smart-ass reply out. I kiss her deep and slow, letting my hands wander down her sides, over the curve of her hips, and back up to her breasts.

She arches into my palms the second I cup them, her breath hitching when my thumbs brush over her nipples. They harden instantly under my touch, and I do it again, rolling them gently between my fingers, learning how sensitive they are all over again.

"Goddamn," I murmur, moving lower, my mouth replacing my hands. I kiss and suck one nipple, my tongue flicking the tight peak until she's squirming under me, then I move to the other, giving it the same attention while my hand slides down between her legs.

She's already soaked, slick, and ready for me, and when my fingers slip inside her, her back arches off the bed, her breath catching on a soft moan.

"Scott," she whispers, her fingers curling in my hair.

"Yeah?"

"I want you inside me."

I kiss my way back up to her mouth, taking my time, tasting every inch of her before I settle between her thighs. My cock slides through her slickness, teasing her clit, and her hips buck, chasing more.

"Patience," I whisper, even though my own is hanging by a thread. "Gotta make sure you're ready for me."

"I'm always ready for you."

She's right, but still, I slide just the head inside, watching her face, watching the way her lips part, and her brows pull together at the stretch. She's so damn tight around me, every time feels like the first time, and I swear I see stars. "Fuck, sugar," I groan, easing in another inch. "You're squeezing me so tight."

"You're just so damn big," she pants, her nails digging into my shoulders. "I need all of you, though. Don't hold back."

I give her what she wants, pushing in slow and steady until I'm fully seated inside her, buried so deep I swear I can feel her heartbeat against my cock. We both go still, just breathing each other in, letting our bodies remember exactly how to fit together.

"Move," she whispers, her hands sliding down to grip my ass.

I do, pulling back almost all the way before thrusting in deep again, watching the way her breasts bounce with every movement. I lean down, sucking her nipple into my mouth again, loving the way she cries out, her body tightening around me like a fist.

"You feel so good," I murmur, moving faster now, each thrust rocking her up the bed, her thighs gripping my sides. "Always so good for me."

She pulls my mouth back to hers, kissing me like she needs me so that she can breathe, her body meeting every thrust, taking everything I give her and asking for more.

Her body goes tight, her moans turning breathless and high-pitched, and I know she's right there, ready to fall.

"Come for me, baby," I whisper. "Let me feel it."

She does, her body clenching so tight around me I nearly see stars, her cries filling the room, and it's all too much. I thrust deep one last time, spilling inside her with a groan, my forehead resting against hers, our breath tangling between us.

We stay like that for a long moment, bodies still joined, hearts still racing. Eventually, I roll to the side, pulling her with me, and she curls into my chest, her fingers tracing lazy circles over my heart.

Milo snuffles from the living room, and Harper giggles softly. "Guess we kept him awake."

"He'll get used to it," I say, pressing a kiss to the top of her head. "That pup's part of the family now."

15

THE SECOND-STRING QUARTERBACK

Harper

Flying with Damien never stops feeling opulent. The jet is sleek and perfect, just like everything he owns. The leather seats are softer than my actual bed, and the flight attendant knows my drink order before I even ask.

Damien's beside me, dressed too well for travel, effortlessly handsome in that "I own the world" way that still leaves me slightly breathless.

I sip my champagne, curling my legs under me as the clouds drift past the window. "So, just out of curiosity, what do you think regular people do when they want to visit their boyfriend in another state?"

Damien grins, stretching an arm across the back of my seat. "I have no idea."

I laugh, leaning into him, the bubbles already fizzing pleasantly in my bloodstream.

Before long, we've landed and made our way through town to Levi's Stadium. The place is loud and alive, fans decked out in red and gold, chanting and waving banners. Damien's private box is, as always, the best seat in the house.

Rafe looks incredible on the field, focused, confident, every movement pure muscle memory. It's a close game, which makes it both more exciting and anxiety-inducing. When Rafe's team pulls off the win, I'm on my feet, bouncing and shouting like an over caffeinated cheerleader.

"He's going to love seeing you here," Damien says, fingers tracing idle patterns on my knee.

I grin. "That's the plan."

After the game, I expect Damien to escort me directly to see Rafe, but instead, he stands abruptly, adjusting his cufflinks.

"Where are you going?" I ask.

"Business," he says smoothly. "It won't take me long. Stay put. Rafe will be here soon."

The box feels too quiet after Damien leaves. The roar of the crowd has died down, replaced by the hum of cleanup crews and the faint echo of footsteps in the halls outside. I check my phone. No messages from Rafe yet, but I know he's probably still in the shower, washing off victory sweat and adrenaline.

I wander around the box, nervous energy twitching in my fingers, until a soft click sounds from the door. I turn, expecting Rafe. But it's not him.

It's Jeff McNaught.

Every muscle in my body locks up. He closes the door behind him, leaning against it with that same too-familiar smirk he wore at the party. "Well, well," Jeff drawls. "All alone, huh?"

I swallow hard, forcing a smile. "Rafe will be here any second."

Jeff shrugs, stepping closer. "Relax. I'm just being friendly." He's too close, his cologne sharp, his eyes glassy with something I don't trust. "I think we both know you've got a thing for quarterbacks. And I've heard you like to share," Jeff continues, his gaze raking over me like he's stripping me bare. "So why stop at one?"

My skin crawls, but I hold my ground. "Get out."

"Come on, Harper." His fingers brush my arm, and I jerk back like I've been burned. "Don't be like that."

I open my mouth, to yell, to scream, to say something, but before I can, the door swings open hard enough to slam into the wall. I've seen

Rafe angry before, but this is something else entirely. His whole body is coiled with fury, his jaw clenched so tight I think I can hear his teeth grinding. "What the hell do you think you're doing?" His voice is low, dangerous, and I actually see Jeff flinch.

"Relax, man," Jeff says, raising his hands like this is all some big misunderstanding. "We were just talking."

"Talking?" Rafe steps between us, effectively blocking me from Jeff's view. "That's what you call cornering my girlfriend? Putting your hands on her?"

"We're just getting to know each other," Jeff tries, but his voice trembles.

"I'm going to make this very simple for you," Rafe says, his voice like steel wrapped in fire. "If I ever see you near Harper again, you won't just lose your spot on this team, I will make sure you can't even walk onto a football field ever again."

Jeff swallows hard. The room is silent, save for my own ragged breathing. Jeff lingers just a second too long, like he wants to argue, but something in Rafe's expression must convince him that's a terrible idea because he turns and leaves without another word.

The door closes behind him, and my knees finally give out. Rafe catches me before I hit the floor, pulling me into his chest, his hand cupping the back of my head.

"Are you okay?" His voice is softer now, but there's still a fury of anger underneath.

"Yeah." I breathe. "I'm fine."

He tilts my chin up, scanning my face, like he needs to see it for himself. "I'm so sorry," he says. "I should have been here sooner. He won't come near you again. I swear it."

I believe him. We sit on the couch for a while, my head resting on his shoulder, neither of us speaking.

"Want to go home?" he finally asks.

"Yeah."

"Okay."

He stands, pulling me up with him, his fingers laced tightly through mine, and together, we leave the box behind. On our way out, we run into Damien, who lets us know he's got a charity event tonight. I want to ask him what took him so long, why he left me alone, but now isn't the time. We tell him goodbye and head back to Rafe's place.

In the car, I lean against him, my body tired but safe, my heart full of gratitude and love and a tiny flicker of fear that I shove deep down. We've made it through worse than Jeff McNaught.

Rafe

Harper sits on the edge of my bed, one leg tucked under her, wearing nothing but one of my old T-shirts. It swallows her up, falling off one shoulder, and somehow, she looks even more beautiful like this than she did in that knockout dress she wore to the game. I can't stop looking at her.

It's been too long since I had her in my space, where I can reach out and touch her anytime I want. And now that she's here, I can't decide if I want to hold her close and never let go, or lay her back and make up for every second we've been apart.

"Are you sure you're okay?" I ask, leaning against the door. "With Jeff, I mean."

She glances up, smiling just a little, but there's something flickering behind her eyes, that tiny shadow that tells me she's downplaying whatever really happened. "I'm fine," she says, brushing it off the way she always does. "Maybe he just got confused? Wrong box or something."

I could press her. Should press her. But not tonight. Tonight is about her. About us. So I cross the room, sitting beside her, letting my hand rest on her bare thigh. "If you're sure."

"I am." She leans into me, her head fitting perfectly against my shoulder, and just like that, my world rights itself.

We sit at my small kitchen table, eating Thai straight from the containers, passing spring rolls back and forth, stealing bites from each other's plates like we've always done. Harper tells me about the gallery in Chicago, the new studio Damien got her, the way she and McKenzy have been staying up late, painting, building furniture, and making magic together.

Her whole face lights up when she talks about it, her hands moving through the air like she's already painting right here in my kitchen. I don't understand half the terms she uses, but I hang on every word because nothing makes me happier than seeing her this passionate.

She pauses, chopsticks halfway to her mouth. "Enough about me. How's the team? How's California life?"

I shrug. "Team's solid. Coaches are good. But honestly?" I set my container down and reach across the table for her hand. "All I've really been thinking about is you."

Her smile goes soft, her fingers threading through mine. "I missed you too."

After dinner, we curl up together on the couch, wrapped in a 49ers blanket, half-watching some comedy we've seen a dozen times. Harper fits against me perfectly, her head on my chest, her fingers tracing absent shapes on my stomach.

Later, I lead her back to my room. We undress each other slowly, hands mapping familiar territory, lips relearning all the places that make the other sigh. It's not hurried, not frantic. It's a gentle kind of worship, a quiet *I missed you* spoken without words. Her hands skim my chest, lingering over old scars and new ones, her fingers warm and familiar, like she's reminding me that I'm not just a football player to her. I'm *me*.

I push her T-shirt up, my thumbs brushing over her soft stomach, up to her breasts. Her breath catches when my palms cup her, my thumbs brushing across her nipples until they pebble under my touch.

"You're so beautiful, sugar," I whisper, leaning down to kiss her neck, her collarbone, the top of her breast. "I don't tell you that enough."

She smiles, pulling my mouth to hers. "Tell me now."

I do, between every kiss, every touch, every slow slide of skin on skin. I tell her she's gorgeous, perfect, mine, until her breath hitches, and her nails dig into my back.

I lay her back against my pillows, spreading her out beneath me, and she opens for me like it's the most natural thing in the world. My fingers trail down her stomach, teasing her inner thighs before sliding between her folds, finding her already slick and ready for me.

"Rafe," she whispers, her hips lifting into my hand. "I need you."

I settle between her legs, guiding the thick head of my cock to her entrance. Even after all this time, she's still so damn tight around me, and I swear I see stars when I push inside, inch by inch.

Her legs wrap around my waist, her heels digging into my lower back, pulling me deeper until there's nowhere left to go.

"Fuck, Harper." I groan, my forehead pressing to hers. "You always feel so fucking good."

She clings to me, her fingers twisting in my hair, her breath warm against my cheek. "Don't stop," she whispers. "Don't ever stop."

I move slowly, savoring every thrust, every slick glide of her body welcoming mine. She rocks her hips up to meet mine, gripping my shoulders like she needs something to hold onto, and I can feel her body tightening around me, every little gasp and moan telling me how close she is.

Suddenly, she breaks apart under me, her body trembling, her mouth falling open in a silent cry.

The sight of her coming around me pulls me over the edge, my release spilling deep inside her, my breath ragged against her neck as we both ride the aftershocks together.

I stay inside her, my weight braced on my elbows, not ready to break the connection just yet. I brush her hair back from her face, kissing her softly on the forehead, the cheek, the corner of her mouth. "You're my favorite person," I whisper because saying anything else right now would be too much.

She smiles, soft and sleepy. "You're mine, too."

We fall asleep tangled together, skin to skin, our hearts still beating in the same rhythm.

HARPER

I WAKE UP ON MY LAST MORNING AT RAFE'S PLACE WITH MY FACE pressed into his chest, the scent of his skin warm and familiar. The sun filters through the window, casting a soft glow over the room, and for a minute, I just lay there, pretending that we always wake up tangled together, with no flights to catch or time zones between us.

But the reality is, I'm heading back to my San Francisco apartment in a little while, and then Damien and I are going back home. Rafe stirs beside me, his arm tightening around my waist, and I close my eyes, savoring the moment a little longer before reality pulls me away. Saying goodbye to him is too difficult, so I put it off as long as I can.

Eventually, it has to happen though. We part ways, and I catch a ride the few blocks to my own place. By the time I let myself into my apartment, Damien is already there, stretched out on my ridiculously plush couch like he owns the place. To be fair, of course, he actually does own the place.

"You look radiant," he drawls, eyes sweeping over me as I drop my bag. "Must've been a good weekend."

I roll my eyes, but I can't help but smile. "Rafe's happy, so I'm happy."

"Adorable," Damien says, sitting up. "Come tell me all about it."

"Actually, there's something else I need to tell you about," I say, my fingers twisting in my lap.

Damien's eyes narrow slightly, his focus sharpening like a predator sensing prey. "Go on."

I tell him about Jeff, the way he looked at me the first time Rafe introduced us, his creepy comments at the party, and the way he cornered me in the box after the game. Most unsettling is how he insinuated that I should try him out since I'm already dating four men.

"Why the hell didn't you tell me sooner?" Damien demands, looking furious.

"Because I don't want to make trouble for Rafe," I say quickly. "This is his team, and I don't want to create drama."

Damien snorts. "Sweetheart, that's not drama. That's called protecting yourself from a certified creep. Jeff McNaught is a walking lawsuit," he says, his lip curling in disgust. "He's been benched for more reasons than just his shitty performance. The guy's got a file full of allegations from harassment to inappropriate behavior, and even a couple of under-the-table settlements."

My stomach twists. "Seriously?"

Damien nods. "And that's not even the worst of it."

I blink. "There's worse?"

"He's been trying to convince some members of the team to throw games," Damien says, "betting against themselves so they can cash in on illegal earnings."

My brain stutters to a stop. "But don't professional football players already make millions?"

Damien's smile is cold. "Greed doesn't have a ceiling, little bird. Some guys get addicted to the rush, the thrill of making money where they shouldn't. And McNaught's exactly the kind of scumbag who thinks he's untouchable. Besides, he's not making the big bucks now that he's been replaced as the starting quarterback."

My stomach churns. "Does Rafe know?"

"Rafe knows some of it," Damien admits. "But I handled most of it before it could touch him directly. I told McNaught in no uncertain terms that Rafe, and the rest of the team, weren't going to be part of his side hustle. And if he ever tried to pull Rafe into it again, I'd make sure the only thing he's throwing is a case in federal court."

I sit with this for a while, and we move on to lighter topics. Before going to bed, Damien tells me he intends to spend the rest of our time here spoiling me. Spoiling me, as it turns out, involves a lot of shopping, drinking, and expensive food. Damien takes me to the kind of stores where the salespeople offer champagne the moment we walk through the door.

I try on everything he picks out, some of it so extravagant I laugh out loud, but Damien just leans back in the plush chair like a king surveying his kingdom, his predatory smile widening with each outfit.

"That one," he says when I emerge in a slinky black dress that clings like sin. "We're definitely keeping that one."

"Where would I even wear this?" I ask, turning in the mirror.

Damien's eyes flash. "It doesn't matter where you wear it as long as it ends up on my bedroom floor."

16

SELF-DEFENSE LESSONS

Scott

The house feels too quiet when Harper's not here. Even with Milo chasing his tail in the living room and the soft hum of the radio in the kitchen, it's not the same. There's no burst of laughter from the next room, no clatter of her paintbrushes or the sound of her humming off-key while she raids my fridge.

I knew when we started this wild, unconventional, what-the-hell-are-we-even-doing relationship that Harper would never belong to just me, and I accepted that. Most days, I'm fine with it. But when she's in San Francisco, it's impossible not to feel like I'm missing a part of her. Still, that's my problem, not hers.

So the second I hear she's back in town, I text her.

Me: Dinner at my place? Home-cooked. I promise.

Her response comes almost immediately.

Harper: Does this include puppy snuggles? Because I miss Milo. (And you, I guess.)

I laugh out loud, shaking my head.

Me: I'll allow it. Be ready at six.

When she slides into my truck, Milo goes ballistic, wiggling all over the backseat, his paws scrambling to get closer to her.

"Hi, baby!" Harper squeals, practically crawling over the console to rub his ears.

"Hey," I say dryly. "Nice to see you, too."

She grins, her eyes sparkling. "Oh, you're here? I didn't even notice."

I fake a wounded gasp, placing a hand over my heart. "Cold, Ward. Real cold."

She leans over, pressing a soft kiss to my cheek. "Hi, baby."

"Hi, baby," I echo.

And just like that, my world shifts back into place. When we get home, the house feels warmer, brighter, and fuller. Milo follows her from room to room, his tail wagging so hard it smacks into the furniture, and Harper talks to him like they've been best friends for years.

"Did you miss me? Were you a good boy for Daddy? Did you eat all your kibble and chase all the butterflies?"

Milo yelps out a high-pitched bark in response, and Harper beams at him like they're having a full conversation. I watch from the kitchen, stirring sauce on the stove, wondering how the hell I got so lucky to have this tiny, chaotic ray of sunshine in my life.

"So," I say over dinner, "how was California?"

Harper sighs dramatically, twirling her fork through her pasta. "Oh, you know. Fancy restaurants, ridiculous shopping trips, billionaires being billionaires."

I grin. "Sounds terrible."

"It was," she says with mock seriousness. "I barely survived." She pauses, her smile fading just slightly. "Actually, there was… one thing."

I set my fork down. "What happened?"

She tugs her bottom lip between her teeth, a sure sign she's nervous. "Rafe's teammate," she says slowly. "Jeff McNaught."

I frown. "The creep who was eyeing you at the party?"

"Yeah." She pokes at her pasta. "He, um… he cornered me in the private box after the game."

I grip the table tightly until my knuckles turn white. "What did he do?"

"He just–" She shrugs like she's trying to make it smaller than it was. "Maybe he was drunk. Said some gross things. Got a little too close."

I push my chair back, already mentally planning a trip to San Francisco just to knock some sense into the guy.

"Rafe handled it," Harper adds quickly. "He walked in and scared the shit out of him. Told him if he ever came near me again, he'd make sure Jeff never plays another snap of football."

"Good," I say, my jaw still tight. "Because if Rafe hadn't, I would've."

She reaches across the table, covering my hand with hers. "I'm okay, Scott. I promise."

I take a slow breath, forcing myself to ease up. "It's a good thing I taught you how to fight."

Her smile turns wicked. "You wanna practice again? I particularly enjoyed how the last round ended."

I smirk at her, and we clear the dishes. In the living room, I push the coffee table back against the wall, and Harper kicks off her shoes, standing barefoot on the hardwood.

"Show me what you remember," I say, arms crossed.

She takes a stance, a little too wide, a little too eager, but damn if she doesn't look adorable trying to be tough.

"Palm strike," I prompt.

She lunges forward, her palm snapping out and catching me square in the chest.

"Good," I say, stepping closer. "Elbow strike."

She spins, her elbow brushing my ribs, and I grab her wrist, pulling her against me.

"Too slow," I murmur.

Her breath catches, her chest pressed to mine. "Maybe you're just too fast."

"Groin kick," I whisper.

Her knee lifts, brushing dangerously close to exactly where it's supposed to land, and for a second, I wonder if she's actually going to do it. Instead, she hooks her leg around mine, flipping us both so we land hard on the floor, her body sprawled across my chest.

"Pinned you," she says, grinning triumphantly.

I flip her instantly, pressing her into the floor, my hands pinning her wrists above her head. "I let you win."

"You're full of shit." She laughs, squirming beneath me.

The movement rubs her body against mine, and just like that, the air shifts from playful to something else entirely.

"Harper," I murmur, leaning closer. "You trying to seduce me, little fighter?"

"Maybe," she whispers back.

I kiss her, deep and slow, my body settling between her legs as her thighs part for me.

Milo barks once, from the corner, like he's scandalized, but neither of us stops. I chuckle as she twists, flexing beneath me, testing my grip. But I'm bigger, stronger, and I use my body to keep her right where I want her.

She likes this. I can tell by the way her breathing changes, by the way her nipples harden against the fabric of her tank top, by the way her hips roll, pressing against me just right.

I let her go. The second I do, she takes control, shoving me backward and climbing onto my lap, straddling me.

"There she is," I tease, sliding my hands up her thighs.

"Cocky," she says again, but she's already rocking against me, grinding slow and dirty against my cock, which is aching beneath my jeans.

"You love it." I grip her hips, guiding her movements, my thumbs pressing into her soft skin.

She's not wearing a bra, and when I sit up and slide my hands under her tank top, her body melts into mine.

"Take it off," I say, already tugging at the hem.

She lifts her arms, letting me strip the fabric over her head, baring all that perfect, soft skin. I groan, cupping her full, gorgeous breasts in my palms, running my thumbs over her already hard, needy nipples.

She gasps, arching into my touch.

"You like that?" I murmur, my mouth already heading south.

She barely has time to answer before my lips close around one of those tight peaks, my tongue flicking slow, teasing strokes until her whole body shudders.

"Scott," she gasps.

I switch to the other one, sucking a little harder, tugging gently with my teeth, and her nails dig into my shoulders as she grinds against me harder.

"God, you're so fuckin' sexy," I groan, kissing my way back up to her lips.

She reaches between us, unzipping and tugging my jeans down just enough to free my cock, and the second my thick, aching length springs free, her breath catches.

I lift my hips, letting her position herself, watching as she slides just the tip inside, her slick heat teasing me, torturing me.

"Fuck, Harper," I grit out, my hands gripping her ass. "You gonna take all of me, baby?"

She leans in, lips brushing my ear. "Every. Last. Inch."

Then she sinks down in one slow, perfect motion, and I swear I see heaven.

I groan, gritting my teeth as she takes me so deep, her body stretching around me, adjusting to my size. She's tight, so fucking tight, and she rolls her hips like she knows exactly what she's doing to me. She starts slow, lifting herself almost all the way off me before slamming back down, making me curse under my breath.

"Fuck, sugar," I groan, gripping her hips, helping guide her movements. "You ride me so damn good."

She's in control, setting the pace, working me over with long, deep strokes that have my whole body tensing. I let her move how she wants, let her fuck me slow and sweet, her hands splaying across my chest for balance, her head falling back as pleasure takes over.

And damn, I love seeing her like this. Totally uninhibited. Totally mine.

I sit up, wrapping an arm around her waist, holding her close as I kiss her slow and deep, my other hand sliding between her thighs, finding her clit. She gasps into my mouth, her body tightening around me, her nails scratching down my back as her rhythm starts to break.

Her whole body shakes in my arms, her head dropping to my shoulder, her moan muffled against my skin as she milks my cock with every pulse of her orgasm.

The way she squeezes me, clenching tight around me, is all it takes to send me over the edge too. I thrust up into her, burying myself as deep as I can, coming hard inside her, holding her tight as I ride it out.

When it's over, we collapse right there on the floor, panting, sweating, tangled up together.

HARPER

BY THE TIME I GET HOME FROM SCOTT'S, MY HAIR'S A MESS, MY LEGS are sore in the best way, and I still smell like his soap and puppy breath. McKenzy sits on the couch, her laptop balanced on her knees and a paint-splattered mug in her hand. The second I walk in, she grins knowingly.

"Well, well," she drawls, "look who just got thoroughly laid."

I drop my bag, flopping dramatically onto the couch beside her. "When am I not thoroughly laid these days?" I joke.

She sniffs the air. "Is that Scott's soap? God, Harper, you're basically wearing his cologne like a hydrant a dog peed on."

I swat at her, laughing. McKenzy closes her laptop, giving me her full attention. "Okay, spill. What's going on in that overworked brain of yours?"

I stare at the ceiling for a second, trying to untangle the mess of thoughts swirling in my head. "I was thinking maybe Scott's not actually looking for more."

McKenzy raises an eyebrow. "Oh?"

"Maybe I've been reading too much into it," I say, waving my hand vaguely. "I mean, compared to Damien, Tomas, and Rafe? Scott's life is calm. There's no ex-wife screaming at me in a parking lot. No mafia vibes. No long-distance football drama. He's just normal."

McKenzy leans forward. "And you think that's why he's more attentive? Because he has the bandwidth for it?"

"Exactly!" I sit up, warming to the theory. "He's not getting pulled in a million directions like the others. It's not that he wants something exclusive. It's just that he can actually show up for me in ways they can't."

McKenzy makes a hmm sound, and I can tell she's holding back.

"What?" I nudge her knee with my foot. "Spit it out."

She shrugs, too casual. "Or maybe, hear me out, it's not that Scott wants to be monogamous."

"Okay?"

"Maybe it's that you want to be monogamous. With him."

I burst out laughing. "McKenzy, I'm literally with four different men right now. That doesn't exactly scream monogamy."

McKenzy shrugs again, but this time her smile has a knowing edge. "No, but you were always monogamous before. With Rafe the first time and then with he-who-shall-not-be-named. Face it, you do act different with Scott."

"What's that supposed to mean?"

"Nothing bad!" she says quickly. "It's just with Damien, it's all luxury and danger. With Tomas, it's all passion and a little bit taboo. With Rafe, it's this epic second chance romance."

"And with Scott?"

"With Scott, it's just… life."

I blink in confusion. "What?"

McKenzy's smile softens. "You know. Normal stuff. Puppies, home-cooked meals, and helping him pick out compost bins for his farm. You two fit in this domestic little bubble, and it's kind of adorable."

I stare at her—because she's not wrong. Scott and I have this ease between us. We could spend an entire weekend doing absolutely nothing and still have a great time. It's terrifying and also kind of beautiful.

"Okay," I admit, grabbing one of McKenzy's throw pillows and hugging it to my chest. "Maybe I do like the whole domestic bliss thing with Scott. But that doesn't mean I want to give up the other guys."

She takes a long sip from her mug. "Or maybe you just don't want to admit you could be happy with only one."

I roll my eyes, even though my heart skips a beat at the truth of it.

"Harper," she says, setting her mug down. "You're allowed to want something simple. It doesn't make you boring. And it definitely doesn't mean you're betraying the others."

I hug the pillow tighter. "I don't know if I can do simple anymore."

She tilts her head. "Because of them or because of you?"

I groan, flopping onto my back. "Why are you always so wise when I'm vulnerable?"

"It's my curse," she says dramatically, and we both burst out laughing.

We stay up way too late after that, sitting cross-legged on the couch, talking about everything and nothing.

McKenzy brings up old college stories I'd rather forget, and I tell her about the time Damien bought an entire restaurant because the hostess told him there were no tables available.

"God, your life is ridiculous," she says, shaking her head. "It's like living inside a Bravo show."

Eventually, we get around to the serious stuff again.

"Do you think Scott knows I'm this conflicted?" I ask softly.

She shrugs. "Scott knows you. And I think he knows that loving you means sharing you."

That makes my chest tighten because it's true, and yet, unfair all at once.

17

A SOUR MELODY

My third cup of coffee sits half-finished on the table, paint still clinging to the edges of my nails from a morning spent lost in my latest piece. McKenzy's out running errands, the apartment is quiet, and I'm riding the kind of creative high that only comes when everything just clicks.

I'm about to dip my brush into a streak of deep teal when my phone buzzes. I grab it without thinking, expecting McKenzy or Scott or maybe one of the guys.

It's the gallery in Chicago.

My stomach flips.

"Hello?" I answer, trying not to sound like someone who just inhaled a cinnamon roll while juggling a paintbrush between her teeth.

"Harper! It's Stephanie at the Whitney." Her voice is bright, almost bubbly. That's already a good sign.

"Hi!" I tuck the phone between my ear and shoulder, scrambling for a notepad in case I need to write anything down.

"I hope I'm not interrupting, but I wanted to call personally,"

Stephanie says. "We've had some really wonderful interest in your work after that last sale."

I clutch the notepad to my chest, heart racing. "Really?"

"We were actually hoping you'd send another piece or two for the next show," she continues. "Nothing formal yet, but there's definitely buzz."

Buzz. For my art.

My voice comes out a little too high-pitched. "That's amazing! Of course, I'd love to."

We go over the logistics, deadlines, shipping, dimensions, and by the time we hang up, I'm floating. This is really happening. My work isn't just sitting in my corner of the studio anymore. It's out there, being seen, being bought, being wanted.

I'm halfway to the kitchen to celebrate with more coffee when my phone rings again.

I glance at the screen, and my stomach plummets, my high instantly crashing.

Mom.

I freeze, my thumb hovering over the decline button.

It's been months since we last spoke. After the whole disaster with Jack, when they wanted me to settle down with him despite his abuse, they pretty much wrote me off. Then, when my relationship status went from "it's complicated" to "try explaining this to your Southern Baptist parents," I figured the silence would be permanent.

Except, ever since my kidnapping, my mom's been texting me every couple of weeks. Nothing deep, just short check-ins, little prayers, polite updates about church bake sales and Bible study groups. I've ignored most of them, but she's been persistent.

But some stupid part of me, the part that still wants a mom even after everything, makes me answer at the last second. "Hello?"

"Harper." Her voice is clipped, but softer than I expected. "It's been a while."

I swallow hard. "Yeah."

We don't exchange pleasantries. That's not how we operate.

"We were thinking it might be nice if you joined us for lunch," she says. "Your father, Melody, and me."

My stomach churns. Melody. Just hearing her name makes my skin crawl. My former best friend who may as well be my parents' daughter instead of me, even though she lied about sleeping with Rafe all those years ago, the one who ruined everything just because she couldn't stand that I had something she wanted.

"We understand if you're busy," my mom adds, her voice slipping into its signature guilt-coated tone. "But we'd really appreciate the effort."

Translation: We're trying to be good Christians by giving you a second chance. Don't embarrass us by saying no.

I press my hand to my forehead, already feeling the headache coming on. "Okay. When?"

I SHOW UP AT THE RESTAURANT TEN MINUTES EARLY BECAUSE BEING late would just give them one more thing to criticize.

It's exactly the kind of place they love, with dark wood paneling, piano music playing softly in the background, a dress code that makes me feel like my tattoos are practically screaming for attention.

The hostess looks me up and down when I walk in, and I can already tell she's deciding if I'm worthy of one of their white linen tables. I resist the urge to stick out my tongue. I'm about to text McKenzy with a live play-by-play of the passive-aggression Olympics I'm about to endure when the door swings open behind me.

My parents walk in first, Dad looking stiff and uncomfortable in his sport coat, Mom holding her purse with both hands like someone might snatch it even though we're in the suburbs. They each give me the kind of hug you offer a distant relative you barely remember, polite, quick, completely devoid of warmth.

Then there's Melody. She's still taller than me even in my heels. Her blonde hair and makeup look effortlessly pretty, but she looks tired. Her skin's pale, her hair's flat, and her eyes dart around the restaurant like she's expecting to be judged.

Six months pregnant and abandoned by her baby's father. That's what mom told me on the phone. She's hardly showing, but she's definitely carrying more weight than usual. She's wearing a flowy dress meant to conceal her situation, so I probably wouldn't notice if I didn't already know.

I shouldn't feel bad for her. But I do.

"Harper," she says, forcing a smile that doesn't quite reach her eyes. "You look… well."

"Thanks." I adjust my sleeve, covering the edge of one of my tattoos. "You look pregnant."

Her smile flickers, just for a second, and I know I scored a hit.

The actual lunch is awkward, but not for the reasons I expected.

I was braced for a sermon on sexual purity or a subtle interrogation about my personal life, but they barely even ask about me. All their attention is locked on Melody's train wreck, how her boyfriend vanished, how her real parents abandoned her, how she had no choice but to beg my parents for a place to stay, who let her move in because, apparently, a baby cancels out being a whore when it's not your flesh and blood.

The hypocrisy makes me want to laugh and scream at the same time, but I bite my tongue.

Mom keeps saying things like, "We're so blessed to have a chance to help Melody through this," and, "Every baby is a gift from the Lord."

It's surreal, watching Melody squirm under this kind of attention. And then, just as I think I might survive this meal unscathed, my mom folds her napkin, sets it beside her plate, and says, "It would mean a lot if you helped with the baby shower."

I blink. "What?"

"You've always been so responsible," she says. "And poor Melody has no one else."

I glance at Melody, expecting her to roll her eyes or snap some insult, but she doesn't.

She just stares at her plate, shoulders stiff, her face carefully blank. For the first time in my life, Melody looks small. And damn it, I feel bad for her. "I'll think about it," I say, and we get back to other topics. Not ones I'm interested in, but at least it's not the baby shower.

When lunch is over, I make it exactly four steps out of the restaurant before I hear Melody's voice behind me.

"Wait."

I close my eyes, exhaling hard through my nose, then turn around, plastering on the most neutral expression I can muster.

"What's up?"

She stands there, her arms crossed over her tiny bump, her expression stuck somewhere between defensive and defeated. Her once-perfect manicure is chipped, her lip gloss is smudged, and the tan she used to be religious about maintaining has faded into the same kind of washed-out exhaustion that clings to her whole vibe.

It's weird seeing her like this, like the queen of perfection finally cracked at the edges.

"I didn't want to say this in front of your mom and dad," she starts, her voice softer than usual, "but I need help."

Melody asking for help? From me?

She rolls her eyes at my silence. "Don't look so shocked. I know you're probably dying to say 'I told you so,' but can you just—" she sighs, hands cradling her belly. "Can you just not?"

It's disarming, seeing her like this. Vulnerable. Almost human. "What kind of help?" I ask cautiously.

"The shower," she mutters, staring at the sidewalk like it's personally offended her. "I have no one else to plan it. Everyone I used to be friends with either drifted off or chose his side."

His. The baby's father. The one who bailed the second Melody's pregnancy test turned pink. Even her fake friends jumped ship.

Part of me wants to gloat. After all, this is the same woman who slept with my fiancé, or at least lied and said she did.

"For real, Mel? You have no one else?"

She lifts her chin, defensiveness flashing again. "I have plenty of people who'd come. But no one I trust to actually handle it."

And that's when it clicks. She's not asking me because she suddenly wants to bond. She's asking me because I'm the only one who won't sabotage her out of spite. It's transactional, like everything in our relationship has always been. But despite all of that, despite every betrayal, every nasty comment, every passive-aggressive swipe she's taken at me since we were kids, I feel this stupid pang of pity.

Because, deep down, I know what it feels like to be abandoned by the people you thought would stand by you. And no matter how much she deserves it, it still sucks to watch.

"Okay," I say quietly. "I'll help."

Her head snaps up, like she wasn't expecting me to say yes without a fight. "Seriously?"

"Seriously." I fold my arms, mirroring her stance. "But I'm not doing it for you. I'm doing it for the baby. He deserves one person who isn't a total train wreck."

Melody's face twists, like she wants to argue, but she doesn't. She just nods. "Fine."

We stand there in awkward silence, neither of us sure what comes next. Eventually, I trudge off, leaving her in my wake.

At home, McKenzy's already waiting with wine and snacks, her feet propped on the coffee table, a knowing smirk on her face. "Well?" she asks, handing me a glass before I even sit down. "Was it the disaster you expected?"

I flop onto the couch, taking a long sip. "Less disaster, more soap opera."

McKenzy perks up. "Ooh, details."

By the time I'm done, we've both drained our glasses and started eating cheese directly from the block.

"Damn," McKenzy says, mouth full. "Your former friend never fails to deliver the unbelievable."

"Right?" I lean my head back, closing my eyes. "And now I'm planning my evil ex-friend's baby shower, like some kind of twisted Hallmark movie."

"Maybe it's not that twisted," she says, nudging my foot with hers. "Maybe it's a fresh start."

I snort. "Or maybe it's a slow-motion train wreck with pastel decorations."

She raises her glass. "To pastel train wrecks."

I clink my glass against hers, not entirely sure if I'm toasting or mourning.

18

BIG IDEAS

McKenzy's perched on top of a step stool, paintbrush clenched between her teeth, holding two wildly different knobs up to a half-finished dresser. One is sleek brass, the other shaped like a ceramic lemon.

"I'm thinking weird fruit motif," she says around the brush. "Or is that too quirky farm wife?"

"Knowing you," I say, smearing cobalt blue across my latest canvas, "it's exactly the right amount of quirky farm wife."

She grins and tosses the lemon knob into her tool bag. "Perfect. If Scott hates it, I'll tell him to take it up with my creative genius."

The studio feels especially bright today, sunlight spilling through the windows, illuminating the organized chaos we've turned it into. My corner smells like oil paint and turpentine. McKenzy's side smells like sawdust and wood stain.

McKenzy spins on her stool, eyeing my painting. "That's new."

"Just started it last night," I say. "It's about Melody. Sort of."

She leans closer, frowning slightly. "It's angry."

"It's complicated," I correct.

"Sometimes they feel the same," she points out.

I wipe my hands on a rag and sit on the edge of the worktable.

"It's weird, you know, seeing her like that yesterday all broken and desperate. I've never seen her like that before."

McKenzy doesn't say anything right away, just lets me talk, which is exactly why she's my best friend.

"Our entire friendship before she pretended Rafe cheated on me seems fake now," I start, though McKenzy more than knows about my ex-best friend drama. "Then there was all that bullshit with Rafe. I honestly don't think I could ever truly forgive her for that. And then she dragged Jack back into my life and tried to implode all of my relationships. And I really thought I'd never forgive her for that. Now, I don't know."

"She's been a big part of your life," McKenzy states sympathetically. "Of course you'll have complicated feelings, no matter what she does. Just know that I'll support you no matter what you decide."

We work in silence for a while after that, both of us lost in our own worlds, me in the mess of color and memory, McKenzy sanding down an old nightstand like it personally insulted her.

Eventually, she breaks the silence. "You know what we need?"

"An espresso machine?"

"Besides that."

I shrug. "A miracle?"

"No." She jumps off the stool, spinning in place. "An art show."

I blink. "What?"

"We have this beautiful space, all this amazing work piling up, and no one's seen it except us." She throws her arms wide. "We should do a gallery night. Open house style. Invite everyone we know, and especially everyone Damien knows."

I laugh. "You just want an excuse to flirt with Damien's fancy art friends."

"Duh," she says. "But also, we'd sell a ton of stuff. And you could show off your new Chicago pieces before you send them to the gallery."

It's a good idea.

A really good idea, actually.

McKenzy's been saying for weeks that my Chicago sale was just the beginning, that if I really want to make a name for myself, I need to put my work in front of more people. And what better way than to throw our own party?

"We could get Damien to blast it all over his socials," McKenzy continues, already spinning with plans. "You know he has, like, half the art world following him. And if he makes it sound exclusive, people will eat it up."

I grin. "We're really doing this, huh?"

"Hell yes."

My phone buzzes just as we're finishing our celebratory second round of peanut butter and cocktails.

It's Tomas.

"Hola, Profe," I say, cradling the phone between my ear and shoulder.

"Hola, bonita," Tomas replies, his voice warm and familiar. "I was thinking. Would you like to go back to the jazz club with me tonight?"

I smile, my stomach doing that stupid little flip it always does when Tomas gets sweet on me. "I'd love to."

"Perfect. I'll pick you up at eight."

When I hang up, McKenzy's already wiggling her eyebrows at me. "Date night?"

"Jazz club," I confirm.

"Fancy."

I shrug. "Tomas and I need a drama-free night."

McKenzy leans back against the counter, her grin turning mischievous. "Are you bringing pepper spray?"

"What?"

"You know," she says innocently. "Just in case Carmen decides to make another guest appearance."

I groan, dropping my head into my hands. "Don't jinx me."

"Hey, I'm just saying. Be prepared."

Back at the apartment, I dig through my closet, trying to find something that says 'I'm sexy but also capable of defending myself if your psycho ex shows up.' I settle on a blue dress that hugs all the right places, paired with very stabby heels, just in case.

McKenzy surveys me as I step out into the living room. "You look hot. Tomas is gonna lose his mind."

"Let's hope that's the only thing anyone loses tonight."

TOMAS

HARPER AND I ARE DANCING IN THE JAZZ CLUB, AND SHE'S DRIVING ME absolutely wild. Every time she rubs herself against me, I'm sure I'm going to explode.

"If you keep that up," I murmur against her ear, "we're going to have to find somewhere private."

She tilts her head, baring her neck to me. "Is that a promise?"

I swear under my breath, tugging her off the dance floor and down the hallway toward the bathrooms.

"Tomas!" she says with a laugh. "What are you doing?"

"Finding somewhere private."

The bathroom is empty, thank God, and I lock the door behind us before pushing her up against the sink. Her laughter turns breathless, her hands reaching to tug me closer.

"Profe," she teases, "this is so scandalous, even for us."

"I swear I was a model citizen before I met you," I shoot back.

I kiss her then, hard and hungry, hands rucking up her dress to find bare skin underneath. No bra, no panties, no fucking way.

"You planned this," I accuse her between kisses.

"Guilty," she gasps.

Her hands work at my belt, my zipper, until she has me free and throbbing against her thigh. She gently strokes me, but I desperately need to feel her warm lips around my cock. I catch sight of myself in the mirror, and I suddenly have an even more scandalous idea.

"Turn around," I order, spinning her to face the mirror. "I want you to watch."

She moans softly and complies, bracing her hands on the sink, legs spreading just enough to invite me in. I pull her panties aside, feeling her slick heat as I guide myself to her entrance.

"Profe," she whimpers. "Por favor."

Her eyes meet mine in the mirror as I thrust into her in one smooth motion. I watch her reflection as she goes wide-eyed and breathless.

"Look at yourself," I murmur, one hand gripping her hip, the other sliding around to tease her clit. "Watch how beautiful you look when I'm inside you."

Her head falls back against my shoulder, lips parted as I move inside her, slow at first, then faster when she pushes back to meet me.

"More," she begs. "Faster."

I give her what she wants, fucking her against the sink until the mirror fogs with our breath and her moans echo off the tile walls.

Her nails scratch against the porcelain, her body tightening around me as she falls apart, gasping my name like a prayer. I follow moments later, filling her with a groan that vibrates in my chest. We stay like that for a beat, catching our breath, my forehead pressed to her shoulder.

"We're terrible," she says, but she's smiling.

"The worst," I agree, tugging her dress back down and fixing my pants.

She smooths her hair, cheeks flushed, lips swollen. "Let's get out of here before someone hears us."

I laugh, unlocking the door and peeking out. "Coast is clear."

Back at the table, we finish our drinks, pretending nothing happened, though my hand stays on her thigh, my fingers tracing the edge of her lace panties.

On the drive home, she curls her fingers through mine, singing softly with the radio.

"You're trouble," I tell her again.

"I had some bad influences in college." She winks.

I can't argue.

"Well, at least one terrible influence," I murmur, remembering that Carmen was her Spanish 102 professor. "And speaking of, I'm glad La Diabla didn't show her face tonight."

"The restraining order must be working," she agrees. "I think she got the message."

"I'm honestly a little disappointed. It would have been priceless for her to see us walking out of the bathroom together."

"She might have murdered me right there." She laughs nervously. "It's for the best."

"I would have protected you," I tell her, brushing a strand of hair behind her ear. "You can count on that."

She kisses my fingertips one by one, pulling each slightly into her mouth. She's driving me crazy, and she knows it. Just as my dick twitches in my pants, she pulls away, a devilish grin on her face.

"I really should go," she whispers seductively in my ear.

"Maybe you're La Diabla," I tease, looking down at my semi-hard on.

"I just want to leave you wanting more," she says with a wink, getting out of the car.

"As if I don't want you constantly," I murmur to myself in Spanish as I watch her walk toward her building.

19

CHAOS AND BEAUTY COLLIDE

Harper

I'm practically vibrating with excitement when I burst into the apartment, nearly knocking poor McKenzy off the couch. She's got paint in her hair, a bowl of popcorn balanced on her lap, and her laptop open to some DIY tutorial. The moment she sees my face, her eyes go wide.

"Okay, what's got you bouncing off the walls like a caffeinated squirrel?" she asks, grinning as she sets her popcorn aside.

"We're doing it!" I practically sing, spinning in a circle. "We're having our art show. And it's going to be huge."

McKenzy gasps and leaps off the couch to grab my hands. "Shut up. Are you serious? How did this happen?"

"Damien," I answer, breathless from my impromptu happy dance. "I mentioned it to him, and before I could even finish the sentence, he had this whole plan. He said he's going to blast it all over social media and call in favors from every art critic, influencer, and high-society snob he knows."

McKenzy's jaw drops. "Holy shit. You know what this means, right?"

"That we actually have to make a ton of new art so we don't look like amateurs?" I laugh, already mentally cataloging which pieces I'm willing to part with.

"No," McKenzy says, shaking her head with exaggerated seriousness. "It means I need a new dress."

We dissolve into giggles, but my phone buzzing in my pocket pulls me back to reality. I fish it out and see Damien's name flashing across the screen.

"Hey, handsome," I answer, flopping onto the couch while McKenzy grabs her laptop and starts hunting for dresses online. "McKenzy and I are officially freaking out, by the way."

"You should be." Damien's smooth, self-assured voice fills my ear. "It's going to be the event of the season, little red bird. Every important name in the Midwest art scene is going to be there. And I've arranged for a couple of national critics to attend, too."

My heart skips a beat. "Are you serious? Damien, that's—"

"Don't thank me yet," he interrupts. "You and McKenzy need to make sure the studio is perfect. I'm sending over a cleaning crew, catering, and a bartender. And I'll have a security team there just in case anyone gets too rowdy."

My stomach flips. It's really happening. "You're incredible, you know that?"

"Of course I do," Damien says, smug as ever. "Oh, and one more thing. I thought you might like to know. Jeff McNaught won't be bothering you anymore."

I sit up straighter. "What? What happened?"

"He got caught gambling," Damien says with a satisfied chuckle. "The coach suspended him indefinitely, and made sure his suspension includes a full ban from the stadium and all team events. He won't be anywhere near you next time you go to one of Rafe's games."

Relief crashes over me so fast I sag against the cushions. "Thank God. I didn't realize how much that was hanging over my head until just now."

"Now you can focus on what really matters," Damien says. "Like your art show. And maybe what you'll be wearing when you thank me later."

I roll my eyes, even though he can't see me.

After I hang up, I share the Jeff McNaught news with McKenzy.

"Well, that's one less creep to worry about," she says, pulling up a sequined dress on her screen. "Now, should I go classic black or slutty gold?"

"Why not both?" I grin. "Slutty with a touch of sophistication."

THE NEXT MORNING, I WAKE UP TO FOUR TEXT MESSAGES. ONE FROM each of my men.

Rafe: So proud of you, sugar. Can't wait to see your work. I'll fly back for it, no matter what. **Scott:** I knew you'd be famous one day. I'll bring a whole crew from the farm. Get ready for a cowboy invasion.

Tomas: My talented preciosa. I want the first private tour before anyone else arrives.

Damien: This show is going to be legendary, little red bird. I hope you're ready for the spotlight.

I hug my pillow to my chest, overwhelmed by the outpouring of love and support.

Later that day, we head to the studio to start setting up. McKenzy cranks up a playlist full of upbeat girl-power anthems while we rearrange furniture, measure walls, and debate the perfect flow for the evening.

"We should do a section that's just collaborations," McKenzy suggests, hanging upside down off a ladder. "Like, a corner that's all the stuff we made together."

"That's a great idea." I'm already imagining a little plaque: *The McKenzy & Harper Collection: Chaos & Beauty Collide.*

Halfway through rearranging our supply shelves, Scott calls. I put him on speaker. "Hey, cowboy," I chirp. "You're live with McKenzy."

"Howdy, ladies," Scott's deep, cheerful voice fills the room. "I was just calling to see if y'all need me to build anything for the show. A display wall? Easels? I can whip up whatever you need."

McKenzy clutches her chest dramatically. "Why are you the perfect man?"

"Trust me, I'm far from perfect," Scott admits. "Seriously, though, let me know."

We make a list of little things we could use—extra shelves, some rustic display crates, maybe a reclaimed wood guest book stand. Scott promises to have them ready in a few days.

"Your harem is really pulling out all the stops for this," McKenzy says after we hang up. "You know how lucky you are, right?"

"I do." I glance around the studio, imagining it full of people, full of my art. "Are we actually ready for this?"

"As ready as we'll ever be," she says, grabbing my hand m and squeezing.

THE STUDIO SMELLS LIKE FRESH WOOD, PAINT, AND POSSIBILITY WHEN Scott strolls in with his tool belt slung low on his hips and a canvas bag of hardware in his hand. This man can even make hanging picture hooks look sexy, and I'm already kicking myself for getting distracted before we even get started.

"Hey, cowboy," I greet him, standing on my tiptoes to kiss his cheek. "Ready to play handyman?"

Scott grins, his eyes sweeping across the studio like he's mentally measuring every wall and calculating every angle.

"More than ready. You got some work gloves for me, or should I just roll up my sleeves and look manly?"

"You know damn well you're not wearing gloves." I smirk. "The whole point is for me to ogle your forearms."

"Good point." He flexes dramatically, and I swat his arm. "All right, show me where you want these hanging systems."

I lead him to the back wall, the longest uninterrupted stretch of space in the studio. "I want a row here for the larger canvases, and then some smaller hooks above it for mixed media pieces. McKenzy wants her heavier furniture pieces against the opposite wall."

He nods, already in full project mode.

"Easy enough. I brought my laser level. We'll get it perfectly straight."

As he unpacks his tools, McKenzy bustles around, rearranging her latest sculpture, an abstract piece made from salvaged wood and twisted copper wire. The three of us work together, chatting and laughing, while Scott drills and measures and generally acts like he was born to make my life easier.

It takes us a couple of hours to get everything set up the way we want it. By the time we step back to admire our work, the sun is setting, and the studio is bathed in a golden glow. My paintings look stunning, even half-hung and slightly crooked. The space feels alive, humming with possibility.

"Well," McKenzy says, hands on her hips. "I'd call this a successful workday."

"Couldn't have done it without you guys," I say, grateful beyond words for my little makeshift family.

McKenzy grabs her bag and waves on her way out. "I'm grabbing tacos with my sister. You two lovebirds can finish up without me. Try not to desecrate the art."

Scott winks at me as the door closes behind her. "Well, now that she's gone…."

"Behave," I warn, even though we both know I'm hoping he won't.

We wander around the studio, making little adjustments, straightening frames, and debating the placement of a sculpture in the corner. But the more we move, the more I feel Scott's eyes on me, and the harder it gets to concentrate.

"Do you know how sexy you look in this space?" he asks, stepping up behind me and sliding his hands around my waist. He kisses my neck, his beard scraping deliciously against my skin. "I love seeing you in your element. You're so passionate when you talk about your art. It turns me on."

"Everything turns you on," I tease him, but my breath hitches when his hands slip lower, tracing the curve of my hips.

"Only when it comes to you." He spins me around, pressing me against the wall we just finished hanging paintings on. "You know what we have to do now, right?"

"Clean up?" I pretend to be clueless, even as my body heats from the anticipation already crackling between us.

"Christen this place." His voice is low and rough, and my knees go weak.

"You want to have sex in my studio?" I try to sound scandalized, but the truth is, the idea is already making me throb.

"Don't you?" Scott's grin is wicked. "First time for everything."

I laugh softly, but the sound dissolves into a moan when he kisses me deep and hungry, like he's been waiting all day for this. His hands slide under my shirt, tracing the skin of my lower back, making me shiver.

"No one's going to walk in, right?" he asks between kisses.

"Nope. McKenzy and I are the only two with keys, and I think she's got the hint."

That's all the encouragement he needs. I reach for his shirt, tugging it over his head, running my hands down his strong chest and stomach. His skin is warm from all the work we've done, his muscles taut under my fingers. "You're so damn sexy," I murmur, and Scott's smile is pure mischief.

"Right back at you, sweetheart." He pulls my shirt off, then my bra, cupping my breasts and thumbing my nipples until I'm writhing against him.

I hook my fingers in his belt loops, dragging him closer. His jeans are already undone, his cock hard against my stomach.

"You came prepared."

"I've been thinking about this all day," he admits, sliding my leggings down my legs, leaving me in just my panties. "You. Me. Right here."

"Tell me." My voice is breathy, needy.

"I imagined you bent over your work table," he growls, gripping my ass and lifting me onto the nearest flat surface. "Or spread out on the floor, covered in paint."

"Let's make those fantasies come true," I whisper, wrapping my legs around his waist.

He kisses me again, slower this time, his hands roaming my body, learning every inch of skin like it's the first time. There's something deliciously naughty about being naked in my studio, surrounded by my own creations.

Scott's mouth travels down my neck, across my collarbone, and lower still. He kneels in front of me, pushing my thighs apart and kissing the inside of my knee, working his way inward until his mouth is exactly where I need it.

I arch against him, fingers tangling in his hair as his tongue works its magic. He knows me so well by now, knows exactly how to make me melt. My back arches off the table, and I bite my lip to keep from screaming his name.

"Scott, please," I beg, desperate for more.

"Not yet." He stands, pulling me against him, his cock sliding against my slick heat. "I want to make this last."

He lifts me off the table and carries me to the floor, laying me down on a drop cloth like some kind of living canvas. I giggle, but the sound turns into a gasp when he sinks into me in one slow thrust.

"Oh, my God." I breathe, clinging to his shoulders.

"Feel good?" he asks, his forehead pressed to mine.

"So fucking good."

We move together, slow and sweet at first, then faster as desire takes over. I rake my nails down his back, leaving little red marks, and Scott groans in response.

"You drive me crazy," he mutters, kissing me hard.

"Good." I hook my legs around him, pulling him deeper.

Our bodies slap together. The only sounds filling the studio are our moans and the faint creak of the old floorboards beneath us. It's wild, messy, and perfect, just like us.

I come first, clenching around him, and Scott follows seconds later, burying his face in my neck as he groans my name. We collapse in a tangle of limbs, breathing hard, completely spent.

For a long moment, we just lay there, my hair fanned out around me like a halo, his hand resting possessively on my hip. I glance up at the paintings on the wall, my work surrounding us like silent witnesses to our passion.

"Well," Scott finally says, his voice warm with laughter. "I'd say this place is officially christened."

I laugh too, kissing his shoulder.

"Best workday ever."

PAMPERED

Tomas

I know Harper well enough by now to see when stress is eating her alive, even when she tries to hide it behind that bright, brave smile. Her art show has been consuming every spare second of her time, and on top of that, she still acts like Carmen is going to jump out at her every time we're out together.

That's why today is all about her.

She has no idea what I have planned, and the look of surprise when I show up at her door with a coffee in one hand and a bag of pastries in the other makes me feel like I already won the day.

"Buenos días, preciosa." I kiss her cheek as she opens the door, stepping inside before she can protest. "I'm stealing you for the day."

She blinks at me, still in her robe, hair a messy knot on top of her head. "Stealing me? What do you mean?"

"I made an itinerary." I wave a folded piece of paper in front of her face, then set it on the counter. "You deserve a 'you day,' Harper. No painting, no stress. Just you being pampered like the queen you are."

Her smile blooms slowly, soft and a little shy. "That's really sweet, Tomas."

"Get dressed, preciosa. And wear something easy to slip off."

Her brows arch. "Why? Where are we going?"

"You'll see." I wink, stealing a bite of her pastry before she swats me away and disappears to get dressed.

Our first stop is a high-end salon I'd called ahead of time. Harper's eyes go wide the second we walk through the door, taking in the sleek marble counters and rows of glittering nail polish bottles.

"We're starting here?" she asks, her voice a mix of delight and disbelief.

"Yes, mi amor. Get whatever you want." I gesture to the reception desk. "I already told them to give you the works."

"Tomas, this is too much."

"No such thing." I take her hand, threading my fingers through hers. "You do so much for everyone else. Let me spoil you."

She doesn't argue after that, just squeezes my hand and smiles as they lead her back to the shampoo bowl. I sit down in the waiting area and wait as she gets her hair done. Then the receptionist calls me back, and I sit in a chair next to hers as we get pedicures together.

"This might be the best surprise date ever," she says, closing her eyes.

"I'm aiming to set a high bar."

"Mission accomplished."

Halfway through her manicure, as her nails are being painted a shimmery blue, Harper turns toward me, expression thoughtful. "Can I talk to you about something?"

"Of course, preciosa. Anything."

She chews her lip for a moment before speaking. "It's about Melody. And my parents. And I guess my whole messed-up history with them."

I nod, encouraging her to continue.

"I told you my parents and I aren't exactly close, right?"

I snort softly. "That's putting it mildly."

She laughs, but there's no real humor in it.

"Yeah. Well, they called me, out of the blue. Invited me to lunch with them and Melody."

My brow furrows. "Melody... your ex best friend?"

"The very same." She laughs, but I see the pain behind her eyes.

I wait, knowing she needs to say this her way.

"It was awkward," she admits. "They barely asked me anything about my life. Melody is pregnant, apparently, and they've basically become her parents now because her parents don't want to have anything to do with her. "

"Even though they basically disowned you," I recall from one of our earlier conversations.

"Exactly." Harper sighs. "The thing is, I feel bad for her. I do. She made some awful choices, but I know what it's like to feel abandoned by one's parents. And now she's expecting this baby, and she's alone, and she asked me if I'd help out with a baby shower."

I see the war inside her play out on her face, empathy battling hurt, loyalty colliding with self-preservation. "What do you want to do?" I ask softly.

"I don't know," she admits. "I've already agreed to do it, and part of me is fine with that because that baby didn't do anything wrong. And when it arrives, I'll essentially have a little niece or nephew to dote on. But part of me wants to change my mind and call it off. I'm still so hurt by the way Melody treated me. And my parents taking her in…."

"They don't make it easy."

"Exactly."

I reach across the space between our chairs, squeezing her arm. "Whatever you decide, I'll support you. But don't feel like you owe them anything. Your kindness doesn't have to be currency."

Her eyes soften. "I knew you'd say something wise like that."

"It's my job." I lean over and kiss her cheek. "Now, no more heavy talk. This is your day, remember?"

"Right." She smiles, and this time it reaches her eyes. "Okay. No more drama. Just pampering."

From the salon, we head to a cozy little French bistro I found downtown. It has tiny tables, fresh flowers in mason jars, and warm croissants served with homemade jam. Harper orders a mimosa, and I follow suit.

"To you," I toast, raising my glass. "To all the beauty you create, in your art and in my life."

Her cheeks flush. We share a charcuterie board, feeding each other bites of brie and prosciutto, and for a little while, it feels like the world outside this table doesn't exist. It's just us, good food, and soft laughter.

"What about your family?" Harper asks after a while, her head tilted curiously. "I met them at the party, but do they really understand what's happening with us?"

"They know I'm seeing someone special," I admit. "But I haven't gone into details."

"Are you worried about telling them everything?"

I shrug. "My family is traditional. But they also know I've never been that way. As long as I'm happy, they'll come around."

She smiles, but I can see the doubt flickering in her eyes.

"Your family might surprise you too, preciosa," I add gently. "People can change."

"Maybe." She doesn't sound convinced. "Or maybe they'll just keep pretending I don't exist."

"If they can't see how incredible you are, that's their loss," I say softly. "You have a beautiful heart, Helena. That's why this is so hard for you. You feel everything so deeply."

Harper

I look down at our hands, Tomas's fingers warm and steady around mine. "What would you do if you were me?"

He exhales slowly, thinking before he answers. "I think I would try for the baby's sake. Not for Melody, not even for your parents. But for the baby. Innocence deserves a chance."

Tears prick at my eyes, but I blink them back. "You're probably right."

"You don't have to do it alone, mi preciosa," he adds. "I'll be with you every step of the way."

That's when he says something that catches me completely off guard, something so sweet and selfless it makes my breath catch in my throat.

"I could come with you to family gatherings," he offers. "If it would make things easier. If it would help them see you in a different light."

I frown slightly. "What do you mean?"

"I mean," he hesitates, choosing his words carefully, "if they think I'm your boyfriend, your only boyfriend, they might be less harsh. Less judgmental."

It's such a generous offer, but the weight of it sits heavy between us. "You'd really do that for me?" I ask softly.

"Claro." He smiles. "Of course. Your family's opinion doesn't matter to me, but I know it matters to you. If pretending helps, I'll play the role."

It's so tempting to take that easy way out, to let my family believe I'm just a sweet girl with one nice boyfriend. But that's not the truth. And as much as I want to mend things with them, I also want to be honest about who I am. Besides, it will be hard to hide the fact that I'm dating Rafe and Damien since they're often in the tabloids, my picture right along with them.

"It's sweet of you to offer," I say, squeezing his hand. "But I can't hide who I am forever. Eventually, they'll have to accept me, all of me, or they won't. But I do appreciate you wanting to protect me."

Tomas nods, respect in his eyes. "Then I'll be there as your friend. Your lover. Whatever you need me to be."

I lean forward to kiss him sweetly, my heart hammering in my chest because I feel so lucky.

After brunch, we walk through the botanical gardens, his hand warm on the small of my back. We talk about art, travel, and all the places we want to see together. He tells me stories about his childhood, about how his abuela used to sneak him pastries from the bakery across the street even though his parents disapproved of it, and I laugh so hard my stomach hurts.

We end up at a little spa where he'd booked us both massages and facials. I'm absolutely in heaven, and I know I'm going to keep him up half the night to thank him for this perfect day.

Dinner is at his place, tapas and sangria on his balcony, the city lights twinkling below us.

As the warm hues of sunset fade to black, we move inside, the air between us thick with unspoken desire. He pulls me into his arms, and we sway slowly in his living room, no music needed, just the sound of our hearts beating in sync.

"I want you," he whispers, his lips brushing my ear. "Let me show you how much."

We don't make it to the bedroom right away. His hands slide under my dress, lifting it over my head and leaving me in nothing but my panties and his soft kisses. He worships me with his mouth, his hands, his body, slow and reverent, like every inch of me is a canvas he's desperate to paint.

I'm lost in him, the taste of sangria on his tongue, the rasp of his stubble against my skin, the way his fingers trace every curve like he's memorizing me. When he finally sinks inside me, it's like coming home.

"Mi preciosa," he whispers against my lips. "Eres perfecta."

EX-FRIENDS

Harper

I stare at the dining table, wondering if I've overdone it.

I've definitely overdone it.

McKenzy, Melody, and I are the only three having dinner, but I've cooked enough for a small army. Roast chicken, garlic mashed potatoes, a side salad, and fresh bread with this fancy herb butter that McKenzy made sit on the table ready to be consumed. I even baked a peach cobbler because I remember Melody liking peaches when we were kids.

I know it's ridiculous since this is just a dinner to discuss baby shower plans, but my anxiety has forced me to create something that feels warm and welcoming, even if this entire situation is about as awkward as it gets. McKenzy peeks over my shoulder as I straighten a fork for the fourth time.

"You want to tell me why you're acting like you're hosting the damn royal family?" she asks sarcastically.

I snort. "Because I have no idea how this is going to go, and if it's a disaster, at least I can feed her into a food coma," I tell her honestly, laying bare all the thoughts that have been swirling around in my head since I agreed to this.

"Solid strategy." McKenzy grins, bumping her hip against mine. "But you've got this."

Her confidence surges through me, but it only lasts until there's a knock on the door. I wipe my hands on a dishtowel and take a deep breath. It's showtime.

Melody stands on the other side of the door, looking apprehensive and nervous. Her belly is more prominent than the last time I saw her, rounding out under a stretchy blue dress. She's outrageously beautiful still, which really isn't fair. She could at least have the decency to look like shit.

My heart pounds as I remember the last time she was here, when she and my parents were berating me for my life choices. A voice in my head reminds me that she doesn't have the high ground here. I do.

"Hey," I say, my voice softer than I intended.

"Hey," she echoes.

We stand there for an awkward second, neither of us knowing what to say.

"Come in," I gesture, holding the door wide for her. "Dinner's ready."

She comes in, and we sit at the table stiffly, neither of us quite sure what to say to break the tension. We talk about the weather. I ask her about baby names. She tells me she hasn't even thought of any yet because she's so stressed about doing this on her own.

"Still no word from the father?" I ask, gently.

Melody shakes her head, stabbing forcefully at her salad. "He ghosted me the second I told him," she says into her mixed greens. "I should've known better."

She sounds exhausted and afraid, and for maybe the first time in my life, I see my ex-friend as vulnerable. Despite all the shit that's gone down between us, Melody's still human. She seems genuinely terrified by the prospect of becoming a single mother, and it breaks me a little.

"Well," I say, reaching across the table to squeeze her hand. "You're not totally alone."

"What do you mean?" she asks, her eyes cautiously meeting mine.

"I want to be here for you," I tell her honestly, surprising even myself. "I want to support you, however I can. That's why I'm going to plan your baby shower."

"You still want to do that? After everything?" she asks as her lower lip trembles and her voice nearly breaks with emotion.

"Yes," I affirm, my decision fully made. "Despite all the bullshit you've put me through, your baby hasn't done anything wrong. He or she is innocent in all this, so I'm willing to help you."

"I could really use it," she answers with tears in her eyes.

"Great," I say, forcing cheer into my voice. "We can work on the gift registry to start. What do you need? Clothes? A crib? Diapers?"

"Honestly?" she starts, her face flushing. "Everything. Mom and dad are way too embarrassed by the situation to help me, and your parents have been a huge help, like they're truly my parents, but I can't ask them to buy my baby anything.."

Anger flares in my chest, hot and protective. "That's ridiculous. Every mom deserves support from their own parents."

"It is what it is." She shrugs.

"No, it's not," I counter. "And I'm going to start by throwing you the best baby shower ever."

Finally, a smile cracks her face. "Thank you. Harper, I never expected you to want to help me."

"I really want to." And weirdly, I do. Not because I owe her or because I'm trying to fix the past, but because she needs this, and I can do it. "McKenzy and I will go all out. You're getting the baby shower Pinterest dreams are made of."

Melody laughs again, and this time it sounds real. "Okay. Deal." We spend the rest of the evening going over the baby shower plans, and everything falls into place.

After Melody leaves, I'm emotionally wrung out. I collapse on the couch next to McKenzy, groaning dramatically.

"Well," my roommate says, "that was surprisingly not a disaster. I'm really proud of you."

"Thanks," I smile, nudging her shoulder with mine.

But as proud as I am, I can't help but think that I've signed myself up for way more than I bargained for. What the hell do I know about throwing a baby shower? This goes way beyond my capacity. I go into my room to call Tomas.

"Mi preciosa." He answers on the first ring, his voice warm with affection. "How was the dinner?"

"Better than I expected," I admit. "I told her I'd definitely throw her the baby shower."

"Of course you did." He laughs softly. "You have the biggest heart of anyone I know. And now, you deserve a drink. Want to come over?"

There's a softness in his voice that catches me off guard. There's no trace of his usual playful teasing or spicy innuendos. He's being unusually gentle, almost like an actual boyfriend.

I say the only thing I can think to say. "I'd love that."

When I get to his place, he greets me with a kiss on both cheeks and a glass of red wine already poured. We curl up on the couch, legs tangled together, drinking our wine and enjoying the soft candlelight he's lit. Soft music plays in the background, and for a moment, I try to forget about all my stupid drama.

To my surprise, though, Tomas has surprisingly strong opinions about baby showers. "No stupid game where the women eat the chocolate from the diapers," he says vehemently with his nose wrinkled. "And finger sandwiches are no-go. Tapas are much better."

I can't help but laugh, not expecting he'd care a bit about any of this. "You're being so sweet." I sigh, relaxing against his chest.

"Does this surprise you?" he asks, arching a brow.

"A little," I admit. "Not that you aren't always sweet. But you're usually a little spicier."

He chuckles, kissing my forehead. "There's a time for spice, mi preciosa. And a time for sweetness."

We stay wrapped together on the couch while he strokes my hair, and we discuss all things baby shower. It's so domestic, it almost seems boring compared to our other activities. But it's so cozy and comforting, I can't help but feel like our relationship is nearly perfect.

Nearly.

"What are you thinking about?" he asks, a strand of my hair wrapped around his finger.

"My parents," I admit. "They'll be at this stupid shower, and they're definitely going to be judging me for my life choices. For all of this," I gesture vaguely between the two of us and then to the air.

"Let them," he says. "They have no power over you unless you give it to them."

"I know that," I concede. "I just didn't think I would have to face them so soon after everything that happened a few months ago. They were so awful to me. Melody, too. I can't even believe I'm planning this party for her. I still barely believe she's having a baby."

"Thank God it's her and not you, eh?" He grins, and the glint in his eye makes me shiver.

"Exactly," I say, and there's a weight to those words that neither of us acknowledges, but we both feel it. A baby would make our complicated situation much worse.

Eventually I'm pulled out of my baby-reverie by the sound of my grumbling stomach.

"Hungry?" Tomas asks, frowning down at me like the overprotective boyfriend he is.

"Dinner was a long time ago," I admit. "I could go for some late night tapas."

"Now you're thinking," he teases, pulling out his phone and scrolling through a delivery app.

We order takeout, settling on tacos from a late-night taco truck. We eat on the floor on a blanket like it's a picnic, leaning against the couch with a movie on in the background because we don't feel like pulling out plates, and Tomas is worried about spills.

"This is not how professors are supposed to live," he says, mock-serious. "I should be dignified."

"And yet, here you are." I take a bite of my taco al pastor. "Slumming it with me."

"Preciosa," he begins, reaching out to tuck a curl behind my ear, "I'd slum it with you anywhere."

By the time the food is gone, and the wine has settled into my bloodstream, my eyelids are heavy, and my head naturally finds its way to Tomas's shoulder. He curls his arm around me, his fingers tracing lazy circles on my back.

"Stay," he whispers, his voice low and half-asleep already.

"Okay," I whisper back, knowing there's little on earth that could convince me to leave.

We sleepily stand up, stumbling to his bedroom together, and pass out in his bed almost instantly.

THE FIRST THING I NOTICE WHEN I WAKE IS THE OVERLY-CHEERY chirping of birds outside the window. The second thing I notice is Tomas's arm draped over my waist, his fingers curled lightly against my stomach, holding me like I'm something precious.

It's such a domestic, easy kind of intimacy, it makes my heart ache. But it also makes me ache in entirely different ways. I shift slightly, pressing my hips back against his. He stirs, his breath warm against my neck, his hand sliding lower almost on instinct.

"Buenos días," he murmurs, his voice still thick with sleep.

"Good morning," I whisper, pressing back again, just to feel the hard evidence of how much he wants me.

He groans softly, pulling me tighter against him, his lips finding the curve of my shoulder. "You're dangerous, mi preciosa."

"Only with you."

I turn in his arms, my fingers tracing the lines of his face, the stubble rough beneath my touch. He's so impossibly handsome in the morning, when he's not quite awake.

"You're staring," he says, one eye cracking open.

"Can't help it," I murmur. "You're too *guapo*."

"And you're too *bonita*." His hand slides up my thigh, under the oversized shirt I borrowed from him last night. "And too tempting."

"Take advantage of me, Profe," I whisper, my voice light but my body already burning for him.

He flips me onto my back in one smooth motion, his body covering mine, and just like that, the teasing melts into something hungrier.

His mouth finds mine, slow at first, tasting and savoring like the wine we drank last night. He cups my breast, thumb circling my nipple until I arch into him, needing more.

"So preciosa," he murmurs against my lips, his accent thicker in the morning. "So perfecta."

His words slide over my skin like silk, making me shiver beneath him. His mouth follows the trail of his hands, down my neck and collarbone, all the way to my breast until his tongue flicks against my nipple, and I gasp, fingers curling in his hair.

"You're trouble," I whisper, my breath coming faster.

He slides his hand lower, pushing my thighs apart, fingers teasing over my already slick heat. I can't help but writhe against him, so desperate for the delicious friction.

"So wet," he groans, slipping one finger inside me then another.

"You make me this way," I gasp.

He moves down, kissing lower and lower and when his tongue flicks over my most sensitive area, I nearly levitate off the bed. His stubble scrapes deliciously against my skin, the contrast between soft and rough driving me wild.

"Tomas," I whimper, hips rolling against his face.

He doesn't stop until I'm trembling, clenching around his fingers, crying out his name. And even then, he doesn't give me a second to recover. He moves back up my body, his cock already hard and demanding between us.

"Now," I beg. "Please."

"Anything for you, preciosa."

He slides into me in one smooth stroke, stretching me deliciously in ways that wake up my body fully. We move together, slow and sweet, until it's too much, and we're clawing at each other desperately. We chase each other to the very edge. His hand finds mine, fingers lacing tight, grounding me as my body breaks apart beneath him.

He follows, spilling into me with a low groan, his forehead resting against mine. Our breaths mingle in the quiet morning light.

2 2

FUTURE EXPECTATIONS

Scott

Harper's been acting different all afternoon. It's subtle enough that most people would miss it, but I know her too well. She's smiling too tightly, laughing with a little too much energy, fidgeting in the way she only does when she's trying to hide something. I could probably write a field guide to Harper Ward's anxious ticks, and they're all fully on display today.

We're hanging the last of her paintings in the studio, lining up each piece she's created for her gallery showing. Harper's perched on the step stool, holding a canvas while I measure and mark the wall. She's so focused now, she's barely breathing.

"All right," I say, stepping back. "That's level."

"Great," she says, but the smile doesn't quite reach her eyes.

I hand her the hammer, and she drives the nail into place with more force than necessary, her knuckles tight around the handle.

"Okay, what's going on?" I ask, leaning my shoulder against the wall. "Because if you hit that nail any harder, we're gonna end up in the shop next door."

Harper huffs out a breath, brushing her hair back from her face.

"It's nothing. I just have a lot on my plate."

I squat down, catching her eyes.

"You always have a lot on your plate," I point out. "Talk to me."

She sighs, deflating a little, like I punctured a hole in the balloon she's been holding inside her chest. "It's stupid," she deflects, not looking at me.

"I doubt that," I say gently, pushing her hair behind her ear. "Nothing you say is stupid. Just tell me what's on your mind, baby."

She sets the painting down, and her whole body language changes. Her shoulders curl inward, her chin tucks down. Now she's defensive Harper. "I'm just overwhelmed," she says slowly, each word measured. "The art show is huge, obviously, and I want it to be perfect. And then there's the whole thing with Melody and the baby shower."

"Okay." I nod slowly. "That's a lot, but it's not the first time you've juggled a hundred things at once." Her smile is tight, like I'm not quite getting it. "So what's the real thing you're not saying?"

Her eyes flick up to mine, and I see something deep and sad in her endless pools of blue. She's not just defensive, she's guarded. That's new for us. Since we've met, we've always been extremely open with each other. It's what makes this relationship, and all of her relationships, work.

A familiar pang of worry settles in my gut, and I remember how I felt before we got Milo. She was hiding something from me then, too. I assumed getting a puppy was too much, too fast, but that didn't seem to bother her after we met him. Even now, he's running around the studio having the time of his life, and she's been watching him with unbridled joy. The only time all day when she seems herself is when she's interacting with him.

No, this is something worse, and I try to push down my anxiety. I trust her with my whole heart, but maybe that's a mistake. Maybe she wants to pull it out and stomp on it.

I brace myself.

Harper

It's been such a wonderful day, it's hard to change things by answering Scott's question, which will no doubt result in a serious conversation. He knows there's something bothering me, but it's hard to break this spell.

All morning long, the scent of fresh paint and sawdust has hung in the air, mingling with the faint aroma of the vanilla candle McKenzy left burning on the windowsill. It smells like creation, like possibility, like everything this studio was meant to be.

Scott has hummed softly while he works. His sleeves are rolled up, forearms dusted with fine wood shavings, and every so often, I've caught myself staring, my heart tumbling over itself like a lovesick idiot.

The whole time, Milo has pranced around between us, his tiny teeth clamped around a squeaky giraffe. Every time the toy squeals, Scott winces, and I can't help but laugh.

"I swear, he's trying to kill me with noise," he complained on one occasion, though he bent down to scratch his floppy ears as he said it.

"He's perfect," I told him because he is. He's a little ball of chaos that somehow was perfectly created for the two of us.

Scott looked up, his smile soft and familiar. "He's almost as perfect as you."

My heart squeezed. I knew it would be so easy to fall into that smile, to let myself believe that all of this, the puppy, the quiet companionship, the easy warmth, could be enough for me.

Except Scott isn't the only man I care about. Almost from the beginning, it's never just been the two of us. And if he wants that to change, I'm afraid that I'll only disappoint him. That's the thought that's been gnawing at me for weeks, and I know that he can tell. He's always so perceptive. Sometimes eerily so.

Instead of answering him, I slide a painting into place on the newly installed hook, adjusting it slightly until it's centered. The whole time, my mind spins, overthinking like it's my damn superpower.

I need to talk to him. I've been putting it off because of all the what ifs. *What if he says he wants more? What if he asks me to choose?*

What if loving him means losing Tomas, Damien, and Rafe? I'm not sure I'm ready to take that step with him yet. I'm not sure that I'm ready to sacrifice any of them. The thought makes my stomach twist painfully.

Milo yanks the giraffe so hard he flips himself over, landing in an awkward sprawl that sends Scott and me into helpless laughter. The sound is so easy, so happy, and it just makes me more certain that I can't keep avoiding this conversation. I need to know where he stands. Because I care about him deeply, and I can't stand the thought of hurting him. As I look into his eyes, I can only hear the pounding of my heart, and I can't stand it anymore. "I've been thinking a lot lately about what you want. From me. From this."

Scott's face falls, and his brows furrow. "Harper, what's this about?"

"It's just–" I break off, rubbing my hands over my face. "I know you care about me. And I care about you. A lot. But I keep wondering if maybe you're secretly hoping this turns into something more exclusive."

He blinks in surprise. "Exclusive?"

"Like, just us," I say softly. "No Tomas, no Damien, no Rafe. Just you and me. And if that's what you want, I need to know. Because I can't give that to you. And I love you too much to lie about it."

There. It's out. My heart feels like it's trying to claw its way out of my chest, but at least the truth is on the table.

Scott is quiet for a long moment, long enough that I start to panic. Then he steps closer, taking my hands in his big, calloused ones. "Harper," he says gently, "where did you get the idea that I want to change anything?"

I blink rapidly, trying to keep the tears from my eyes. "I just see how easy it is with you, how normal we are together. And sometimes I wonder if you want more of that. Like when we're around your family, I wonder if you wouldn't be happier if we were together for real, and you could tell your parents that we have plans to settle down and start a family or something."

He smiles, shaking his head. "Sweetheart, I'm happy exactly the way we are."

"You are?" My voice cracks, relief and disbelief colliding inside me.

"I knew what I was signing up for," he says. "You were never going to be a one-man woman. And I didn't fall in love with some imaginary version of you who fits in a little box. I fell for the real you, the messy, chaotic, loves-four-men-and-has-a-studio-full-of-paint-splatter-crazy you."

Tears prick at the corners of my eyes, and I laugh softly. "You really mean that?"

"Of course I do." He cups my face, brushing the tears away with his thumbs before they can fall. "I love you, Harper. And I love that you have this huge, complicated heart that makes room for all of us."

I throw my arms around his neck, holding him so tight I can barely breathe. "I love you, too. So much."

We stay like that for a long moment, Milo bumping against our legs with his squeaky giraffe, the whole world narrowing down to just the two of us and a very noisy puppy.

When we finally pull apart, I let out a shaky breath. "God, I've been stressing about that conversation for weeks."

"Why?" He looks genuinely baffled. "Harper, I'm easy. I thought you knew that."

"I guess part of me was scared you'd want what so many other people seem to want–the house, the picket fence, and monogamy–the same normal life everyone else in your family has."

He shrugs. "Maybe that's what I wanted before. But you changed that. You showed me that love doesn't have to look one way. It just has to feel right."

"McKenzy's going to laugh so hard when I tell her this." I groan. "She's been saying all along that I was overthinking everything."

"Well, she knows you pretty well."

"That she does."

We go back to work after that, hanging the rest of the paintings, but everything feels lighter now. The unspoken tension is gone, replaced by the easy comfort that makes being with Scott so damn wonderful.

At one point, Milo grabs a paintbrush and bolts across the room, his tail wagging like a lunatic. Scott chases him, laughing, and when he scoops him up, the brush dangling from the puppy's mouth, I snap a picture on my phone.

"Caption this," I say, showing him the photo.

"'The world's messiest assistant,'" he suggests.

"Perfect."

Later, when we're finished, we sit on the floor with Milo curled between us, munching on leftover pizza McKenzy left in the fridge.

"I love this studio," Scott says, looking around. "It feels like you."

"With a dash of McKenzy," I say softly.

He smiles, leaning against my shoulder.

"Thank you for being so understanding," I tell him honestly, relieved that our dynamic is back to normal finally.

"We're a team, Harper," he says. "Always."

I lean my head on his shoulder, heart full to bursting. "Always."

That night, when I crawl into bed, I send a quick text to McKenzy.

Me: You were right. I overthought everything. Scott is perfect. Also, we ate your pizza. I'll repay you in wine and tacos.

Her reply comes almost immediately:

McKenzy: Told you, bitch. Now go have kinky sex, and let me sleep.

2 3

OLD ANXIETY

Harper sits across from me on the jet, barefoot, her legs tucked up under her like we're on her beat-up couch instead of a leather seat that probably cost more than her apartment. She fits in my world about as well as a paint-splattered easel in a corporate boardroom, yet I still find her absolutely irresistible. I love the way she cracks me open, lets in sunlight where there used to be nothing but polished surface and empty space.

She catches me staring and grins, her hair a messy halo around her face. "What? Did I spill soy sauce on my shirt again?"

"No." I sip my scotch, savoring the burn, the way it sharpens my focus. "I'm just admiring the view."

She rolls her eyes, but there's a blush rising to her cheeks, and it kills me how easily I can get under her skin. No one else blushes for me. Not the models, not the debutantes, not the socialites who'd sell their souls to spend a night in my bed.

Only her.

San Francisco glows under a soft sunset by the time we land, and instead of heading to her apartment, I take her straight to the St. Regis. Top floor suite, of course. Because I can.

169

"Damien," she groans, her fingers sliding over the silk wallpaper next to the massive windows overlooking the bay. "You didn't have to do this."

"Of course I did." I press a kiss to her shoulder, whispering against her skin. "I'm always going to spoil you when I have the chance."

She rolls her eyes, but she doesn't argue. She loves it when I lavish her in luxury, even if she pretends not to.

Dinner is at my favorite sushi place, tucked into a side street most tourists never find. The chef knows me by name, which means we don't even have to see the menu. The courses simply arrive, tiny bites of perfection laid out before us. Each one is more decadent than the last, but nothing is as delicious as watching Harper's reaction to it all.

She closes her eyes with every bite, her little food moans making me hard under the table. I'd pay a fortune to have that sound piped into my office on a loop.

"You know you've ruined me, right?" she says after a third piece of uni melts on her tongue. "I'll never be able to eat grocery store sushi again."

"That's the point." I lean back in my chair, watching her with the kind of hunger that has nothing to do with fish. "Ruining you, that is."

Her smile curves slow and wicked. "I fully expect you to later."

After dinner, I take her to The Fillmore, where one of her favorite bands just happens to be playing. It's a little surprise I set up weeks ago. Although now, I'm wishing I'd just whisked her back to the hotel.

Her face lights up when she sees the marquee, and she's on tiptoe, kissing me hard right there on the sidewalk before we even walk inside. "How did you know?" she asks, breathless.

"I make it my point to know everything about you."

We find our seats, but soon we're on our feet, and she presses herself to my side through the whole set, her body moving to the music. Her hips brush against mine just enough to make me wonder if she's doing it on purpose. By the third song, I'm sure she absolutely is.

Back at the hotel, the air between us shifts the second the door closes behind us.

Harper's smile turns wicked, her hands sliding up my chest, pushing my suit jacket off my shoulders. "I was promised a little ruining tonight, Mr. Blackwood."

"Oh, little red bird," I cup her jaw, thumb tracing her bottom lip. "You haven't seen ruined yet."

She's wearing a slinky black dress that clings to her curves like it's sculpted to her, and I can't decide if I want to strip her out of it or fuck her while she's still wearing it.

"You've been teasing me all day," I murmur, backing her toward the massive bed. "In the restaurant. At the concert. On the jet."

"Maybe I like making you suffer, baby," she teases, her smile sharp and sweet.

"Oh, I'm going to make you pay for that."

Her breath catches when I spin her around, pressing her front to the window overlooking the city. I know she loves doing it like this. She's such a saucy minx; she secretly loves the idea that someone might be watching. But tonight, I want her just for me.

I pull her back toward the living room, until I have her pressed against the back of the couch.

"Bend over," I order. "Spread your legs."

She does as she's told. I slide my hand up her thigh, pushing her dress higher, baring her nakedness beneath.

"You've been a bad girl," I murmur, my fingers finding her already wet and ready as usual.

"I'm sorry, Damien," she purrs. "Maybe you should spank me."

Damn if I don't nearly burst at her words. We haven't tried that before, but I've always wanted to. It's like she read my mind. She looks over her shoulder at me, eyes heavy and expectant. I raise my hand and smack her ass lightly. She grinds herself further into me.

"Now, now, little red bird," I warn. "You can get off when I say you can get off."

A shiver runs through her body and she pivots her hips forward, obedient.

"Yes, baby," she moans. "You should spank me again for my disobedience."

I do, and this time, she stays still, though I don't miss the way she gasps. My other hand sneaks forward, groping at her barely-clad tit and feeling how stiff her nipple is. Fuck, I'm not going to make it much longer, and neither is she.

"Are you ready for me to fuck you, little red bird?" I ask, though I know how ready she is… how ready we both are.

"Only if you think I've been a good girl," she squeaks out.

"Oh, you've been a very bad girl," I hiss in her ear. "I'm going to ruin you for it, remember?"

She shivers again in anticipation, as I undo my belt, my slacks pooling at my feet. I slide into her in one quick thrust. She gasps, her body sagging against the couch, her nails leaving faint streaks in the leather.

"You like this?" I ask, voice low and rough. "Being punished for teasing me?"

She nods, biting her lip.

"Use your words, little bird."

"I love it," she gasps. "Please, punish me harder."

I grip her hips, slamming into her just the way she likes, with the sound of skin on skin. She screams my name, and I clamp a hand over her mouth, bringing her flesh against my chest.

"Shhh," I whisper. "Do you want everyone to know how dirty you are for me?"

She moans against my palm, and it's the most beautiful sound I've ever heard.

I reach around, my fingers finding her clit, rubbing tight circles until she's shaking, her body clenching around me so hard I nearly lose it right then.

"Come for me, baby," I order. "Or else I won't know how much I've ruined you."

She shatters in my arms, her legs giving out, and I catch her, holding her steady as I follow her over the edge. We collapse onto the couch, still tangled together, her breath warm against my neck.

"Fuck," she whispers. "That was–"

"Intense," I finish, kissing her slow and deep.

HARPER

The sun is too bright, and the crowd is too loud, but none of that matters because I'm still riding the high from last night.

I shift in my seat, thighs pressing together as my body remembers exactly what we did against the couch. And then again in the bed. The entire hotel might've heard me screaming, and I can't even bring myself to care.

Now, we sit in our stadium box, and the crowd is alive with energy. Rafe's already on the field, throwing warm-up passes that look effortless even from this far up. He's settled in so much since his first game. Even from here, he looks happy, and seeing him like that makes me happy. If not a little forlorn.

Damien is beside me looking almost bored, but I know better. His attention flickers to his phone, then back to me, then to the field, like he's mentally managing a thousand things at once.

"Are you actually watching, or are you placing bets?" I tease, nudging his knee with mine.

"Can't a man multitask?" His grin is wicked. "I can appreciate your boyfriend's spiral and make a little money at the same time."

"Damien!" I swat his arm, but I'm laughing. "You're terrible."

"Maybe next time you can spank me," he whispers into my ear, and I can't help but shiver.

The game kicks off, and I get swept up in the cheers and chants, the sheer energy pulsing through the stadium. Rafe looks amazing out there, and every time he glances toward our box, I swear his smile gets a little brighter.

"He's showing off for you," Damien mutters with the slightest hint of jealousy, swirling the amber liquid in his glass.

I smile because I know he's right.

The fourth quarter rolls around, and the 49ers are up by ten. Rafe's having a hell of a game, and I'm practically bouncing in my seat, ready to tackle him the second he's within reach. Then Damien's phone buzzes. His expression shifts just slightly, but enough for me to notice.

"I need to step out for a second," he says, standing smoothly.

"Now?" I frown. "It's almost the end of the fourth quarter."

"I'll be back before the game is over," he promises, already halfway to the door.

I grab his wrist before he can go. "Wait. You're not leaving me alone, are you?"

He leans down, brushing a kiss across my forehead. "I'll be two seconds, little red bird. You'll be fine."

I want to believe him, but the ghost of Jeff McNaught lingers somewhere in the back of my mind.

"He's suspended, Harper," Damien reminds me, reading my mind like always. "He's not allowed anywhere near the stadium."

"You said it yourself," I remind him. "He doesn't follow rules."

"And I said I'd be back before you even miss me."

He kisses me again, softer this time, and then he's gone, leaving me alone in the cavernous luxury box with only my own anxiety for company.

I try to focus on the game. I really do. But every time the door creaks or footsteps echo down the hall outside the box, my heart jumps into my throat. It's not that I think Jeff will burst in and drag me out by my hair. He's not Jack, for goodness' sake. But the memory of his eyes on me, the way he seemed to undress me with a glance, still makes my skin crawl.

I scroll through my phone, texting McKenzy about baby shower plans, checking my DMs, doing anything to distract myself from the gnawing worry that Damien's absence will lead to something bad.

Five minutes pass. Then ten.

I press my palms against my knees, bouncing them nervously, trying to remind myself that this is fine. Damien is probably sweet-talking a sponsor, making a shady backroom deal, or whatever billionaires do when they disappear during football games.

24

A SWIFT KICK TO THE NUTS

Harper

I tell myself I'm being dramatic, but even as I try to talk myself down, my hands tremble where they rest on my lap. The air in the private box feels too still, like the whole stadium is holding its breath right along with me.

I hate that my brain goes right to Jeff McNaught. I know he's not supposed to be here. He's suspended, kicked off the premises, and if he so much as buys a hot dog from a vendor outside the stadium, someone will recognize him.

But logic doesn't help. Maybe it's just PTSD, but I'd clocked Jeff as a sleaze the second I met him, and he's done nothing to help that. Our last encounter really left me shaken, and I'm genuinely terrified of facing him again.

As long as the door stays closed, I tell myself I'm safe, even though the game has just ended. Thankfully, the 49ers won. I should go down to greet Rafe, but I decide to stay here and wait for Damien so I'm not navigating the stadium on my own.

More than anything, I'm pissed at Damien for leaving me when he knew I was worried about being left alone again. He sure is in for a spanking later, and it won't be gentle or sweet. He's going to suffer for this.

The door handle turns, and my revenge thoughts are cut short. I turn around to give Damien a piece of my mind, but it's not him. It's a six-foot-five, two-hundred-twenty-pound smirking, entitled bastard.

My stomach plummets, my heart slamming against my ribs so hard it hurts.

"Well, well," Jeff drawls, stepping inside like he owns the place. "Look who just can't seem to stay away."

"What the hell are you doing here?" My voice comes out sharp, but not nearly as steady as I want it to.

He shrugs like this is nothing, like I'm overreacting. "Relax, sweetheart. I just wanted to stop by and say hi."

"You're not allowed here." I stand up, my heart racing faster now. "You're suspended."

"And yet, here I am." His grin sickens me, and I take a step back, my calf bumping the seat behind me. "I couldn't help but notice you've been coming to all of Rafe's home games. It's sweet. It almost makes me wonder if you aren't here for someone else."

I laugh, a sharp, humorless bark. "In your dreams."

"Oh, I've dreamed about you," he says, stepping closer, his voice low. "Wanna know how those dreams end?"

"No," I snap, backing up further. My pulse roars in my ears, my fight-or-flight response kicking in so fast I feel dizzy.

But I've trained for this. Scott made sure of that.

When Jeff lunges for me, reaching for my waist, instinct takes over.

I palm jab him straight in the nose, just like Scott taught me, and there's a satisfying crunch followed by Jeff's startled yelp.

His hands fly to his face, blood already leaking between his fingers, but I don't stop. I drive my knee up, hard, right between his legs. He collapses, gasping like a fish out of water.

Before he can recover, I grab the collar of his shirt, yanking it up and over his head, trapping his arms in the fabric like some kind of makeshift straitjacket.

"Don't ever touch me again!" I shout, my voice shaking with adrenaline as I shove him backward. He hits the floor with a heavy thud, and I bolt for the door.

I don't even think about screaming. I just do it, my voice cutting through the hall like a siren.

"Help! Someone help!" I call as I run out of the box.

I barely make it five steps before I see two very familiar figures sprinting toward me. Damien, all dark fury and expensive rage, and Rafe, still in his uniform, his cleats clattering against the tile.

"What happened?" Rafe grabs my shoulders, his eyes scanning me from head to toe like he's checking for wounds. "Are you okay?"

"I'm fine," I pant, the words tumbling out fast. "It was Jeff. He came in the box and tried—"

Before I can even finish the sentence, Damien is already passed me, barreling through the door like a man on a mission to end careers and break bones.

Rafe's face goes from concern to pure fury in a heartbeat. "Damn it! I had a feeling that fucker was up to something. Stay here."

I grab his arm before he can follow Damien into the box.

"No," I say. "It's okay, I handled it."

Rafe blinks. "What?"

"I handled it," I repeat, my voice steadier now that the adrenaline is burning off. "Ask Scott. He taught me."

Rafe looks at me like I just told him I lifted a car with my bare hands. "You took down Jeff McNaught?"

"Damn right I did." My hands are still shaking, but there's pride in my voice now. "Nose, groin, shirt yank takedown combo. It was beautiful."

Rafe's stunned silence lasts all of two seconds before a grin splits his face. "That's my girl."

Damien emerges from the box, his suit rumpled, his knuckles slightly bloody. I don't ask what happened in there. I don't want to know.

"He'll never bother you again," Damien says, brushing my hair back from my face. "I'll see to that personally."

I believe him.

Security arrives moments later, and by the time they haul Jeff away, one hand still clutching his broken nose, his shirt hanging off like some tragic fashion statement, I'm leaning against Rafe, my knees still a little wobbly.

"He's going to be permanently banned from the NFL for this," Damien says, pacing the hall like a man who needs something else to punch.

"He should've been a long time ago," Rafe mutters.

Damien is a mess, disheveled in a way I've never seen him before. He apologizes to me so much that I finally threaten to give him the "Jeff McNaught Treatment." He laughs humorlessly, but promises me he'll never do it again—or leave me alone.

They leave me with a security guard while they go to talk to the team owner. I don't know all that's said, but I know that Jeff is never going to bother me, or anyone else, ever again.

Rafe

Harper's curled up on my couch, her hair still a little messy from her epic takedown. All I can think about, over and over, is how close we came to something much worse.

If Damien and I had been just a few seconds late.... If Jeff had gotten his hands on her before she could defend herself....

I clench my jaw, the thought sending a fresh wave of anger through me. Harper handled herself, but she never should've had to in the first place.

"You okay over there?" Harper's voice breaks the silence, soft and a little teasing, but I can hear the edge underneath. She's worried about me, even after everything that happened to her tonight.

That's Harper. Always thinking about everyone else, even when she's the one who should be wrapped in a blanket, sipping hot cocoa, and being doted on like the queen she is.

"Yeah," I lie. "Just thinking."

"I'm okay," she reminds me for the millionth time. "And Damien is going to take us all on a very expensive vacation to make up for it."

"That's not the point."

"It kind of is," she says, her voice gentle but firm. "I'm okay because I'm strong enough to handle myself. And because you, Damien, Scott, and Tomas have taught me to be. I'm not some fragile girl you have to protect all the time."

She's right. And I'm so damn proud of her. But somehow, that pride makes me even angrier at myself.

"I love you," she says softly, her face buried in my chest. "Even when you're being hard on yourself."

"I love you, too," I whisper, wrapping both arms around her like if I hold on tight enough, I can erase everything that went wrong today.

We lay there for a while, just breathing each other in, until Harper finally pulls back and gives me a wicked smile.

"Wanna help me wash off the stadium stress?" she asks, her eyes sparkling.

I don't answer. I just stand, scooping her up with me.

She lets out a soft gasp but wraps herself around me effortlessly, her arms linked behind my neck as I carry her into the bathroom.

The second I set her down, she reaches for the hem of her shirt, lifting it over her head and letting it fall to the floor. I let my hands slide up her sides, following the curves I've memorized a thousand times over, and she tilts her head up, her lips already parting for a kiss.

I take my time with it, kissing her slow, deep, like I'm pouring everything I feel for her into the touch of our mouths. She sighs against my lips, pressing closer, and I walk her backward into the shower, letting the hot water pour over both of us.

Her skin is already slick, warm, the steam curling around us, making everything hazy. I reach for the shampoo, squeezing a dollop into my palm before gently working it through her hair.

Harper hums in approval, tipping her head back, trusting me completely.

I take my time, massaging her scalp, rinsing her off, applying the conditioner, rinsing again, then smoothing my hands down her arms, her back, every inch of her. I can't stop touching her. I don't want to stop. When I wrap my arms around her from behind, her breath catches, and she presses herself into me, soft, wet, and perfect.

"I need you," I murmur against her shoulder, my fingers teasing along the swell of her hip.

She lets out a breathless little laugh, then reaches back, threading her fingers into my hair, tilting her head to kiss me over her shoulder.

"You have me," she whispers.

I groan, pressing her against the shower wall, letting my hands roam down her stomach, between her thighs. She's already slick, and not just from the water. I slide two fingers inside her, slow and deep, curling them just right, and she gasps, her nails digging into my wrist.

"Rafe," she moans.

"I've got you," I murmur, my free hand bracing her against me. "Let me take care of you, sugar."

She nods, breathless, thighs trembling as I stroke her just right, my fingers working her open, coaxing her toward the edge. She's shaking against me, her body arching, her lips parting in a silent cry of pleasure. Then she's coming, pulsing around my fingers, her entire body going taut, her head dropping back against my shoulder.

I whisper filthy things in her ear as I hold her while she falls apart. When she finally catches her breath, she turns, her lips finding mine in a slow, needy kiss.

"Bed," she murmurs against my mouth.

I lift her again, carrying her out of the shower, drying her off before I bring her to my bed. I lay her down, climbing over her, settling between her thighs, taking a moment to look at her.

She's flushed, her hair still damp, her eyes soft and full of something I can't name but never want to lose. I brush a strand of hair from her cheek. "You sure you're okay?" I confirm.

She nods, reaching for me. "I couldn't be better." She sighs, pulling me closer for a deep kiss.

That's all I need to hear.

I sink into her, slow and deep, groaning as she stretches around me, hot, wet, and so damn perfect. She wraps her arms around my shoulders as her legs lock around my waist, pulling me closer, like she wants me as deep as I can possibly go. I move slowly, savoring the feel of her, the way she clings to me, the way she sighs my name like it's the only word she knows. She runs her hands down my back, over my arms, like she's memorizing me, too. And when she gasps, arching, nails raking down my spine, I know she's close again.

"Let go for me," I whisper, pressing my forehead to hers. "I've got you, sugar."

She cries out, her body clenching around mine, pulling me over the edge with her, and I bury my face in her neck as I come, holding her as tightly as I can.

Afterward, I stay inside her, unwilling to break the connection just yet. She runs lazy fingers through my damp hair, her lips pressing a soft, almost absentminded, kiss to my temple. "You're coming to the art show, right?" she murmurs.

I huff a laugh, lifting my head to kiss her. "I wouldn't miss it if we were playing the Cowboys, sugar."

"Good," she sighs happily, snuggling closer. "I want you there for all of it. Even the boring parts."

"There are no boring parts when it comes to you," I murmur, letting the words settle between us.

2 5

SHE HAS TO CHOOSE

Harper

The studio is packed, with dozens of people filtering in and out, drinking champagne, admiring the work, and talking in hushed tones. McKenzy stands beside me, her eyes wide as she watches a well-dressed couple argue over who gets to buy one of her handmade pieces.

Across the room, a small cluster of critics and collectors linger in front of one of my paintings, nodding thoughtfully. I feel like I might burst into a thousand bright, brilliant colors all over one of my canvases. After weeks of planning and stressing, we're watching our dreams come true in real time.

Damien, true to his word, has invited half the city... the important half, at that, the art world elite, the socialites, the people with bottomless bank accounts and a thirst for status are walking around our space, bidding for our work. I exhale, trying to ground myself, but McKenzy grabs my arm, squeezing hard.

"Harper," she whispers, "Michael Fucking Vernon is here."

I blink at her, confused for half a second before I follow her gaze. My stomach immediately drops.

Holy. Shit.

It's one thing to run into Michael at one of Damien's fancy parties, but it's a whole other experience to see him walking through our gallery admiring our pieces.

Damien appears beside me, a champagne flute in hand, looking smug as hell. "You're welcome," he murmurs, clinking his glass against mine.

I shake my head, heart racing. "You did this?"

"I made a few calls." He shrugs. "Turns out when I say an artist is worth paying attention to, people listen."

I swallow hard, gripping my glass like it's the only thing keeping me upright. Michael Vernon tilts his head, steps closer, and then he turns….

And walks straight toward me.

"Oh, God," McKenzy whispers. "Breathe, Harper. Don't be weird."

I elbow her sharply, but I do take a quick breath. I could meet Michael Vernon a hundred times and still feel starstruck by him.

"This is an impressive collection, Ms. Ward," he says, nodding toward my work. His voice is deep, measured, like a man who doesn't speak unless he has something worth saying.

I feel like I might pass out. "Thank you," I manage.

He nods once, then leans in slightly, lowering his voice. "Don't let them tame it."

"Tame it?" I echo, confused.

"These people." He gestures vaguely to the well-dressed crowd. "They love to buy art, but they also love to shape it, to tell artists what sells, what works, what fits their aesthetic." He holds my gaze. "Don't let them tell you who to be."

"I won't," I promise, swallowing hard.

A small smile tugs at the corner of his mouth. "Good."

And just like that, he walks away. The moment he's gone, McKenzy grabs my shoulders and shakes me.

"Oh, my God," she whisper/screams.

"I know," I whisper/scream back, trying to maintain my composure and not completely melt into a puddle.

We both squeal quietly before gulping down our champagne,

trying to act like we're not having a full-scale meltdown in the middle of our own show.

As the night stretches on, I find myself orbiting between the four men in my life, each one making my pulse race in very different ways.

Scott hugs me from behind, kissing my temple as he murmurs, "Proud of you, baby." His big, calloused hands are warm against my waist, grounding me in a way only he can.

Tomas, looking entirely too good in his dark suit, smirks when he catches me looking. *"Eres la estrella de la noche,* Helena." *You're the star of the night.* He takes my hand, kissing my knuckles slowly, sending heat straight down my spine.

Rafe, still every inch the golden boy, grins at me over his drink, then leans down, his breath hot against my ear. "Pretty sure half the guys here are wondering how the hell they can steal you from us." His voice dips lower. "They don't stand a chance."

Damien watches me from across the room, his emerald gaze dark with pride, hunger, and something deeper, something only he can feel. When I pass by, his hand finds the small of my back, lingering just long enough to make me shiver.

They're all here, all dressed to kill, making me feel like the luckiest woman alive. There's no way I could have done any of this without their support.

Before the night is over, most of our work is sold. McKenzy's handmade furniture, my paintings, even some experimental pieces we weren't sure would get any attention are gone, claimed, wanted.

When the last buyer leaves, I sink onto one of McKenzy's custom benches, exhaling hard.

She flops down beside me. "Holy shit," she sighs.

"Holy shit," I echo.

We glance at each other then burst into wild, slightly delirious laughter.

"I think we just made a ridiculous amount of money," she says, eyes wide.

"I think we did," I agree.

She grabs my hand, squeezing tight. "We did this, Harper."

We built something from nothing. We took our work, our talent, our vision, and our souls and put them into the world. And the world wanted them. It's every artist's dream to have a night like this, and I feel so lucky that I got to experience with my best friend, and all the men I love the most.

"To us," McKenzy says, holding out an empty hand as we're both too exhausted to actually get up and grab a glass of champagne.

"To us," I echo.

But, as always, my needs have been anticipated as Rafe and Tomas walk over and hand us each a glass. We clink our glasses together and take a sip before reluctantly getting up to tidy up the place. Scott is already busy at work, cleaning up all the trash and collecting the glasses for the caterers.

Damien, unfortunately, had to leave an hour or so ago. He had some late-night business deal he couldn't miss. Typical, jet-setting billionaire stuff. I didn't mind, though. After all he did to make tonight a success, he had every right to leave when he needed to. Before he left, he kissed me long, deep, and dirty, whispering something about celebrating properly the next time I'm in his penthouse.

Rafe and Tomas busy themselves with sweeping and resetting the space while McKenzy starts cataloging all the pieces we sold. The less work we have to do later, the better. I go over to help Scott collect glasses.

"Y'know," he says when I reach him, setting a glass down, "you're kind of amazing for what you accomplished tonight. You pulled it all together pretty quickly. And look at the incredible work that came out of it."

I smirk, leaning on the counter. "You doubted me, Bauer?"

"Never," he says easily, then pulls me in by my waist, pressing a soft kiss to my forehead. "Just proud as hell of you, baby."

Warmth spreads through me, but before I can respond, Tomas appears, twirling an empty wine glass in his fingers.

"Sí, Helena," he agrees, smirking. "You're very impressive."

I arch a brow. "Did you ever question that I was?"

"Never." He steps closer, brushing his knuckles over my cheek.

"But I am wondering how I can convince you to paint something just for me."

Rafe leans against the wall, arms crossed, watching us with amusement. "I dunno, man. You might have to bid for it. I hear her work is selling for high prices these days."

Tomas hums thoughtfully. "Or maybe I'll trade."

"Oh?" I tilt my head. "And what exactly are you offering?"

He leans in, voice dropping just enough to make my breath catch. "Something worth more than any of these buyers could afford."

Scott groans loudly, tossing a towel at Tomas's head. "Damn, can you two flirt after we're done cleaning?"

I laugh, shoving Scott lightly. "Jealous?"

"Hell yeah," he grumbles, but he's smiling.

Rafe rolls his eyes, pushing off the wall. "All right, come on. The sooner we finish, the sooner our girl can rest."

We busy ourselves for another half hour, silently moving through the room to get everything finished. By the time the studio is clean and locked up, I feel bone-deep exhaustion settling in but also an overwhelming sense of peace. Tonight went better than I could have possibly imagined, and the rest I get tonight will be well deserved.

Scott, Tomas, and Rafe linger outside, saying their goodbyes, making plans for later.

"Helena, I'll see you tomorrow, sí?" Tomas murmurs, pressing a kiss to my cheek.

"Sí," I tease, smiling.

Scott squeezes my shoulder, earning a smile from me. "I'll call you after, baby."

"You better."

Rafe is the last to leave, wrapping me up in a long, slow hug, his hands firm on my lower back. "You okay?" he murmurs, his breath warm against my temple.

I nod against his chest. "I couldn't possibly be better."

He smiles against my skin, kissing the top of my head before finally pulling away. "Good. Sleep well, sugar."

And then, just like that, I'm alone.

When I get home, I unlock my phone to check my notifications. I have a flood of messages from buyers, one from Damien letting me know his jet landed, and a TikTok from McKenzy of a goat wearing a scarf. She's already in her room decompressing from the night, and I shoot her a heart reaction. Then my screen lights up with an unknown number. An international number, at that. I hesitate before answering.

"Hello?"

"Alo!" a heavily accented voice calls from the other side of the world. It must already be morning wherever she is because she sounds much more chipper than I feel. "Is this Harper Ward?"

"Yes?" I answer, completely taken aback.

"This is Marianne LaFleur, director of the École des Beaux-Arts in Paris. I apologize for the abrupt call, but I wanted to reach out personally with an opportunity we think you'd be perfect for."

I pull the phone away and stare at it again, like this might be some kind of joke. "I'm sorry, what?"

She laughs a light, airy giggle and says something to someone near her in French. "Apologies, Ms. Ward, I didn't even think to check the time. It must be late there, so I'll keep this brief. We've been following your work," she continues, "and we'd love to offer you a position as a guest instructor at the school for the next year."

My knees buckle, and I sink onto the couch. My mind takes a long moment to process her words, but my heart is already pounding in my chest with excitement. An art school in Paris wants me to teach.

An art school.

In Paris!

They didn't just hear about me, they like my work enough to ask me to teach there.

I press a hand to my chest, trying to breathe through the sudden rush of emotions. "This is amazing," I gasp. "I don't even know what to say."

"You don't have to say anything yet," Marianne says warmly. "Think it over. We'll send the official details to your email. Look it over carefully and get back to me by next week. But Harper?"

"Yes?"

"We really want you here. If the contract isn't up to your standards, we are very open to negotiation."

We exchange a few more pleasantries before we hang up, and I'm left sitting there, staring at my phone. My heart pounds so loud it sounds like roaring in my ears.

The email comes over almost immediately, and I glance over the details. It's a year-long teaching gig, and they're offering a lot of money… too much money, if I'm being honest. McKenzy will lose her shit when I tell her.

I scroll through an attached brochure and can already feel my heart swell, imagining myself strolling the streets of Paris, painting in the shadow of the Eiffel Tower. I know I'm too tired to make any decisions tonight, but I can already see myself belonging there. My art would be featured on a global stage, and I'd have the opportunity to interact with some really incredible young artists.

As quickly as the excitement builds, it falters. A year in Paris would also mean a year away from my studio, from McKenzy, from Tomas, Scott, Rafe, and Damien. Well, probably not Damien. Knowing him, he'd likely fly out to Paris once a week and even rent some fabulous apartment for me.

Still, my life is here. Could I really just pack up everything and leave, even for a once-in-a-lifetime opportunity like this? I glance around the space, at everything I've built, everything I've worked so damn hard for, and a hard truth settles into my chest.

I have to choose.

Thank you for reading! Book 3 is coming soon!